THE BEST OF BOTH WORLDS
VOLUME 1

Edited by Tyree Campbell & J Alan Erwine

The Best of Both Worlds
Volume 1
Edited by Tyree Cambpell and J Alan Erwine

Cover illustration Watchtower by Teresa Tunaley copyright 2016
Cover design by Laura Givens

First printing December 2016

Alban Lake Publishing
Colo, Iowa
http://www.albanlake.com

Nomadic Delirium Press
Aurora, Colorado
http://www.nomadicdeliriumpress.com

Contents

The Best of Both Worlds 2016: Introduction

Once upon a time, the late, great James B. Baker founded a little independent publishing company called ProMart. He envisioned that ProMart would publish good, solid, readable stories by writers known and—to be generous—not so known [this writer included], and incidentally to earn a little dosh on the side. For the most part, he published online, and only in his last couple years did he begin to move on into print. Then he passed away [but watches over us, nonetheless].

One of his print publications was called Wondrous Web Worlds—the title doubtless taken from the fact that it comprised the very best stories he'd published online in The Martian Wave and The Fifth Di…. For the most part, these were science fiction and fantasy. In 2001 he released Vol. 1, which is no longer available; it contained the best stories of 2000, including a few by writers who later won awards [including me]. In 2002, he released Vol. 2, which is available through iUniverse. In 2003, posthumously, he released Vol. 3, also available through iU.

By this time ProMart had become Sam's Dot Publishing. I kept SDP in line, while J Erwine kept it online. We continued Jim's two magazines, and added several others. We also continued, for a while, Wondrous Web Worlds, even though only about 25% of it came from online publications. Eventually, WWW was discontinued, I dropped out for a year or so, and J formed his own publishing company, Nomadic Delirium Press. We continued to work together on sales, and soon I was back, founding Alban Lake Publishing.

J and I have de [hmm…J & I sounds like Men in Black] cided to reconstitute an annual volume of our very best work. First, however, a caveat: All, which is to say, 100%, of the pieces we publish are good, solid, readable material. All good magazines publish this. Obviously, some pieces are better than others, but all are GSRs. So when I write "very best," this in no way denigrates any other pieces. End of caveat.

In honor of both our enterprises, we have decided to call this annual anthology The Best of Both Worlds. You're holding the first edition right now—the best from 2015. We've restricted the material within to stories, and specifically to science fiction or fantasy tales—genres both of us publish. Nomadic Delirium has included stories from The Fifth Di... and The Martian Wave. Alban Lake has included stories from Outposts of Beyond and FrostFire Worlds. J has introduce his selections; in mine, you'll find several stories about dragons, including those folks who communicate with them telepathically; and stories about a witch child who rescues victims from an avalanche caused by demons; a retiree who returns from the dead [yes, it's SF, not Z]; a Reaper who finally meets his match; and a conqueror who would use the knowledge in the last books on Earth to pursue his conquests.

I wouldn't speak for J, but for me the selection process was made almost unbearably arduous by the fact that so many stories were worthy. But as it was said in *Highlander*, there can be only one [per issue].

And now, to borrow from the barker who does the calls in the boxing arena, "Let's get ready to imaginnnnnnnnnnnnnnnnnnnnnnne!"

Tyree Campbell
Alban Lake Publishing
December 2016

The Best of Both Worlds 2016 Introduction

More years ago than I'd like to acknowledge, James Baker and I were working together at ProMart Publishing. We had been publishing on-line and print magazines, and we decided that we wanted to do a best of the Web anthology. Jim left it in my hands, and I came up with the title *Wondrous Web Worlds* (WWW). Jim and I published a few of those until his untimely passing.

When ProMart became Sam's Dot Publishing under the guidance of Tyree Campbell, we continued to publish the annual anthology. In fact, by the time things were said and done, we published ten volumes between ProMart and Sam's Dot.

As is often the case, things happen. Sam's Dot more or less closed its doors, and I began my own publishing company, Nomadic Delirium Press, but Tyree and I kept in touch and as Alban Lake Publishing began, we kept working together in different forms, and finally we came up with the idea of publishing a combined anthology that would feature the best science fiction and fantasy from the magazines that we publish. Tyree already went over the specifics, and the book you now hold in your hands, or that you're reading off of your computer, tablet, phone, or whatever new contraption they've come up with is the result of our work.

As Tyree mentioned, the selection process was difficult to say the least. I could have easily used all of the stories that I'd published in *The Martian Wave* and *The Fifth Di...*, but that wasn't possible, and so I chose these. Who knows, on a different day, my selections might have been different. To avoid any indication of preference, I decided to list the stories in alphabetical order by title. Maybe Volume 2 will be alphabetical by author, but I certainly didn't want to try to pick what would be the best of the best with honors, sir!

I hope that you thoroughly enjoy this collection.

J Alan Erwine
Nomadic Delirium Press
December 2016

The Adventures of Colo Collins and Tama Toledo in Space and Time
By Tyree Campbell

Episode 1: Let's Find Out

Colo Collins and Tama Toledo sat in the old red Datsun pickup and waited for the train to pass. The train was the latest in a series of obstructions regarding their date. First the battery had balked; then the side windows had rolled down of their own accord; finally, Colo had discovered that the restaurant where he'd wanted to take Tama to dinner had closed three weeks ago. And now the train.

"It's okay," said Tama, and patted his hand.

Easy for her to say that, he groused. She'd had limited options; most boys didn't care to date a girl who was twice as intelligent as they were. Unless there were side benefits, and Tama Toledo had never been one for those. That hadn't mattered to Colo, either. He just wanted to go out.

A month ago, as the probable starting quarterback in his senior year, Colo had had a multitude of options. He'd gone out with two or three girls, but none of them had impressed him as great to talk with. Most were artificial, as he'd learned a week later. They sought the selfies and the prestige, not the relationship.

All that had changed the day Colo had walked into Coach Mather's office and announced he was withdrawing from the team. The reason had been simple: sixth-period class for all athletes was Phys Ed, so they could do their warm-ups and have a little extra practice time "off the books." But Honors Physics, which Colo very much wanted to take, was only offered during sixth period.

At first Coach Mather was aghast, then puzzled. Finally he tried to reason with Colo by pointing out that Colo had a decent chance, with the right training and college team, of making it to the NFL. But Colo admitted only to a keen interest in science. "You're a fool," said Mather, and dismissed him.

By the next day, word had gotten out around the school.

Shunned by his former teammates, ignored by girls in general, Colo was cheered only by the light smile on the lips of his Physics teacher. Colo knew he'd made the right decision; it was nice to have it confirmed.

The train passed. The barrier rose.

Colo's thoughts drifted to Tama Toledo, now inviting him to put the truck in gear and cross the tracks. She was at least as intelligent as he was, having demonstrated that in several classes they had shared over the past two years. She was tall, maybe three inches shorter than his six-one, and slender and somewhat gawky on occasion. She had long flaxen hair and bright blue eyes, and thin lips, and an abundance of freckles. He saw all this now. But for two years he had been looking elsewhere.

"The train's passed," Tama said softly.

For the date she had bound back her hair in a ponytail, and put on a black camisole and black jeans. The touch of eyeliner made her eyes glow as she looked at him.

"This isn't going well," said Colo.

"As long as we don't get hit from behind, I'm happy," she hinted.

Still he did not move the pickup. Finally he slapped his hands on the steering wheel. "Jacob Schmidt told me I was un-American," he seethed.

"It doesn't matter what he says," Tama soothed.

"He was my best friend."

"Sometimes you need to lose the friends that need losing, so you can find others along the way."

At first her words slugged him. In another moment, they began to seem profound in some way he could not identify. Taking his laments in stride, she was also taking his part, a subtle whisper to him that he was not alone. His anguish faded, lost in the sound of the idling truck engine. He shifted in gear and drove on toward a place where they served a decent pizza.

"Jacob Schmidt," mused Tama. "He was in my Advanced Chemistry class last year. I'm not sure why. I remember one day Mr. Greene put up a big poster of the periodic table of elements, and Jacob stared at it and stared at it for the longest time. Finally he turned to me and said, 'I can't figure out what day it is.'"

Colo barked a laugh, and coughed. His hands jerked on the steering wheel, but he righted the pickup without difficulty. "That's," he gasped, "that's priceless."

"So maybe you shouldn't worry too much about what he says," said Tama, and pointed. "You could turn left up there," she suggested.

"To Sparkle Vista?" said Colo, surprised. "That's where . . ."

"I know what goes on there," Tama said quietly. "But I just want to look at the stars."

Colo took the turn. "Yeah," he said, feeling the same inclination. His spirits lifted. "I'll honk the horn when we go through DuMont Tunnel."

The narrow road began to wind up a gentle slope, the yellow dividing lines barely visible in the headlights. Forests loomed on either side, great shadowy shapes that seemed to close on Colo and Tama like the pincers of some great black crab. As the pickup rounded a curve, they spotted the tunnel entrance. It bored through the mountain and came out to descend into an agricultural valley below, but off to the right a gravel road led to Sparkle Vista, where the stars provided the only light for those who sought the shelter of the darkness.

Another half mile, thought Colo, as the pickup entered the tunnel. Headlights made a circle of light that pushed through the tunnel ahead of them.

"Honk it," urged Tama.

Colo shook his head. "I'll do it at the halfway point," he told her. "That way we get the effect coming and going. Roll down your window. And . . . *now.*"

Colo sounded the horn, one long beep followed by a series of four short ones.

They heard the horn. They did not hear an echo.

Colo was so startled by the lack of a response to the horn that he almost slammed on the brakes. His brain refused to function; what had not happened was impossible not to have happened. It was as if the tunnel had swallowed up the sound of the horn.

"Try again," said Tama, hushed.

"Insanity is—."

"When you do the same thing over and over and expect a different result," said Tama, somewhat exasperated. "Let's go insane. Try again."

Colo tapped out four short bursts on the horn. The horn sounded as it should. The sounds did not echo.

"Told you," he said.

"We're not the problem," Tama returned. "We're not getting an equal but opposite reaction."

"I doubt Newton applies in this case."

"I don't know what *would* apply." Tama paused briefly, hesitating. "Colo, how long is DuMont Tunnel? Half a mile, right?"

He nodded. "About that."

"Haven't we gone more than half a mile?"

His eyes automatically checked the odometer, uselessly. "I-I . . .Yeah, I think we have. Tama, what . . . ?"

A wisp of fear passed through him. He started to slow the pickup.

"Keep going," she told him.

"We should turn around."

She touched his arm. The intensity in her voice scalded him. "I'm a little afraid, too," she admitted. "But whatever this tunnel is, it has to go somewhere. Let's find out where."

"I don't want you to get hurt."

Tama laughed. "And they say chivalry is dead." Abruptly she sobered. "Whatever it is, we face it together. First rule of science: let's find out."

"Good rule," Colo agreed. "I like that rule."

"As for getting hurt . . . , Colo, whatever this is, they have to know we're here. If they wanted to hurt us, they could have done so already."

Colo brought the pickup back up to speed. "Do you think it's aliens?"

Tama shrugged. "It's someone who has a method of totally absorbing sound," she answered. "Maybe scientists can do that; I don't know. But it's also someone who can seamlessly convert a half-mile tunnel into this, whatever it is. Two miles now, do you think?"

"At least—."

Headlights reflected back at them, slightly warped, as if in a carnival trick mirror. He slowed the pickup to a stop.

"It's a curved wall," he said.

"It looks metallic," added Tama.

"We're blocked. There's no way through."

She nudged the passenger-side door open. "We won't know that until we check it out." She sniffed the air that rushed into the cab. "Smell that?"

"Like hot electrical wiring," was Colo's assessment.

He opened his door and stepped out onto what he assumed was pavement. Instead of asphalt, he found a glassy-smooth surface beneath his feet. In the dim light, the surface looked bluish—the same color, he realized, as the wall itself. The hot electric smell was stronger, but it was not accompanied by heat. The air around him felt pleasantly cool.

He moved to the front of the pickup, where Tama stood waiting for him. He estimated they were about ten feet from the wall. It blocked off the entire tunnel, and seemed to be sealed over the end of it.

"I don't see a door," said Tama. Her voice shook, just once. "Colo?"

"Yeah, I'm still scared, too." He put his arm around her shoulders and gave her a little hug. "Together, right?"

She nodded vigorously. "Together."

They stepped forward until they were within arm's-length of the wall. It was somewhat convex, and the end of the tunnel fit seamlessly against it. Colo started to reach out and touch the wall, but Tama stopped him.

"Wait," she said. "What if . . . if it absorbs you right into it?"

"Follow me," he said.

"Maybe it wants you, but not me."

He frowned. "I wouldn't like that. But what do you suggest?"

"We touch it together," she said.

"Solved it."

They touched the wall. Immediately a door slid to one side with a hissing sound. Tama cried out in surprise. Colo gasped, and drew her back.

"I didn't see that coming," he muttered.

"A door," said Tama, the hint of a giggle in her tone. "How quaint."

The doorway opened to a passageway that led in either direction. Beyond that was a flat wall. The floor of the passageway was pale gray, the wall a cool light blue. On the wall at eye level, in dark blue block lettering in English, was the word BRIDGE, and under that an arrow pointing toward the left.

"I think they were expecting us," said Colo, stepping into the passageway.

"This doesn't look much like Kansas, Toto," said Tama, following.

They turned left. The passageway bent a little to the right and led to a closed door not a dozen steps away. Together, Colo and Tama put their hands to the door, and it slid open. The promised bridge awaited them.

A wide concave window, dark for the moment, curved above what was obviously an instrumentation console. To one side of the console, fixed into the wall, was an array of three monitors without indicated functions. A pair of captain's chairs stood at the console, awaiting occupation.

Behind them, the door slid shut with a *snick* of finality.

"So we're staying here, then," said Colo.

Tama moved to a chair and sat down. "I'm anxious and nervous, but I don't get the sense of any hostility," she said. "Whoever or whatever is behind this simply wants us to do something."

Colo shook his head. "This is so obviously a spacecraft of some kind, Tama. We've been . . ."

"Abducted?" tried Tama.

"More like selected, chosen," said Colo. "So far, we haven't been compelled to do anything. We've proceeded on our own."

"So we're still in 'let's find out' mode?"

He nodded, and sat down, too. "I think we're going to learn by doing," he said.

"On-the-job training. Colo?"

"Right here."

"If we've been selected, we also have the option of turning around and going back to the truck," she pointed out.

Colo looked at her, and met her gaze. In the overhead glow of bridge light, her eyes were royal blue, and deep, as if he might fall into them if he wished. His own, he knew, were gray-green, and he wondered what she saw in them.

"Let's find out, together," he told her.

She nodded once, an emphatic gesture of acceptance.

Colo raised his voice, though he thought it was probably unnecessary. "Hello, ship's computer," he said. "Are you there?"

"Of course. My sensors have confirmed your identities as Colo Collins and Tama Toledo. Welcome aboard this craft."

The voice was a metallic, medium-pitched monotone, like a primitive robot in an older space TV show.

"How were you able to identify us?" asked Tama.

"DNA," answered Colo, before the computer could respond.

"Correct."

Tama's deep frown made her pale eyebrows meet over the bridge of her nose. "But we never gave you—."

"We touched the door," Colo reminded her.

"Oh. Of course."

"What's your name?" asked Colo. "What's the name of this spacecraft?"

"Neither have as yet been named. Naming is your honor."

Colo and Tama exchanged glances. He gave a little nod, and she said, "The name of this craft is the *LetsFindOut*. All one word."

"I can't think of a name for you," Colo told the computer. "Do you have an image or something that might inspire a name?"

"I can choose an appearance that would be aesthetically pleasing to you. Look at the left monitor."

Colo did so just as the face and bare shoulders of Tama Toledo appeared in the monitor. "It's *you*," he said to Tama, laughing.

Tama looked surprised. "*I'm* who you want to see . . . wait a *minute*." She spun the chair to face him. "Am I *naked*?"

Colo held up a hand placatingly. "It's just your face and

shoulders—."

"Put my clothes on *right now!*"

Immediately, in the chair, Colo was wearing a white summer frock and tan, open-toed sandals.

Colo cried out, plucking at the fabric around his chest.

"Omigod!" gasped Tama. "Computer, what have you *done?*"

The metallic monotone resumed. *"I have the ability to dress you for various occasions."*

Tama's laughter overrode her incredulity. "Well, put his clothes back on him, please. And . . . if I'm who he finds inspirational, he can have my face and shoulders in the monitor. But that's *all*, understand?"

The computer restored order.

After a sigh of relief and a stretch of his legs to make sure everything had been restored intact, Colo said, "We should name the computer after the craft, and call her Lettie. Um . . . Tama? You must have seen something different in the monitor."

Tama averted her eyes. "Yeah."

"Who was it?"

"It was—."

"I'll handle this, Lettie," Tama broke in. "Just answer the questions put directly to you. We are quite capable of carrying on our own conversations."

The *"Oh very well"* sounded stiff and huffy, even for a monotone computer.

"It was Legolas," said Tama. "Orlando Bloom."

"Good choice," Colo allowed.

"Colo?"

"Yeah?"

"It didn't occur to me that we could choose each other as our inspirations. I would have chosen you."

"Yeah?"

"Yeah. And now I think I'm very glad that I was your choice. Even with bare shoulders."

He reached his hand out, and they did a little fist-bump.

"Lettie," said Colo, "I don't think we'll need an image in order to communicate with you. But can we do something about your voice? Let's try this: when you speak, let me hear you as Tama, with her tones and inflections, and let her hear you as me. Can you do that?"

"Of course," said Lettie, in Tama's voice.

"Solved it," said Tama.

"And now, Lettie," said Colo, "what's going on? Why are we here?"

"You had to ask," said Tama.

"In the Universe, various events are always taking place," Lettie began. *"The Universe unfolds as it is supposed to, according to the laws of physics—or the Laws of Reality. Some—indeed many—of these events have what might be considered detrimental effects. A tidal wave smashing a forest, for example, or an entire species wiped out. The technology aboard this craft makes it possible to intervene in these events, and change their courses and consequences."*

"So we're to change the natural course of events in the Universe?" asked Tama.

"Yes, and no. I said the changes were possible. You two must decide whether to make those changes. And I do mean you two. You must both agree to make the indicated change before it can be carried out."

"A tie goes to the Universe," said Colo.

"Something like that."

"So we might stop a star from going supernova," mused Tama. "Or help someone find her house key."

Colo shook his head. "Do you realize how crazy this all sounds?"

"As intriguing as this is," added Tama, "I have to agree with Colo."

"Your skepticism is understandable. Might I point out that you are not the only interventionists in the Universe? You are among many."

"Many," repeated Colo. "So there are others like us. Lettie, how did we come to be here? Did you choose us? Did you just spot the two of us on a date and think, yeah, those two will do?"

"I can tell you only that you two were chosen. It is fruitless to pursue this line of inquiry at this time."

"Chosen," repeated Tama. "On what basis?"

"It is fruitless—."

Colo waved his hand in dismissal. "Yeah, yeah, we get it. But you did choose us to change the course of the Universe, right?"

"Changes are requested every day—every minute, every second. Help is requested to locate a house key. An entire population asks for deliverance from a star about to explode."

"You're talking about . . . about prayer," said Tama, hushed now. "You're talking about God."

"Yes, and no. God—whatever you conceive of God to be—is not going to lead Rebecca by the hand to her house key. Nor is God going to throw a stasis field around a star. Instead, assuming an intervention has been approved, Rebecca may see a reflection from a window crystal and look in that direction, below which she will spot her house key on a ledge. Scientists may discover that their calculations regarding the impending supernova are off by, say, four thousand years, giving them more time to develop space travel and escape. Your task is to evaluate the consequences of intervention and non-intervention, and make the decision whether and how to intervene."

Colo got up and began to pace the bridge. "Who approves these requests, these . . . prayers?" he asked.

"That is beyond our level of action."

Tama laughed. "Above your pay grade. But it sounds as if Colo and I have the final decision as to whether to carry out an intervention, as you call it."

"That is correct."

Again Colo waved in protest. "But that would make us gods."

"Yes—."

". . . and no," muttered Tama.

"You may think of it as acting in the stead of God, if you wish. But I assure you that this is how requests are answered. Beyond that, we get into cosmology and metaphysics. Try not to think too deeply on this. Do what your heart and mind tell you is right. No one can ask more than that."

Tama said, "How do we find out about potential interventions?"

"Why, I tell you about them, of course."

"What if we make a mistake?" she asked.

"What you might consider a mistake is part of the way the Universe unfolds and develops. Heart and mind, remember."

Colo looked at Tama. The expression on her face seemed to ask, "Shall we?" He himself still retained doubts. What Lettie was suggesting didn't just push the envelope, it exploded it. He worried about debris, and shrapnel. He had gotten Tama into this by asking her out. He was responsible . . .

Her hand touched his. He had not even been aware that she had moved from her chair. Now she was kneeling on the floor beside him, looking up into his face, his eyes.

"Let's," she whispered.

That was all he needed. "What's first, Lettie?" he asked.

Tama smiled, and rose, and stood beside Colo's chair, her hand resting on his shoulder, listening.

"About eight thousand light-years from here is a world that is going to be struck by a very large asteroid in two days. That's Earth days. You must decide whether to divert the asteroid. In the meantime, Colo, your stateroom is on the starboard side of the LetsFindOut, and Tama, yours is on the port side. I suggest you go to them, arrange them however you wish, have a bite to eat, and get some rest. We'll arrive in about nine hours. Earth hours."

"Wait," said Colo. "What about time dilation? I don't want to come back to Earth and find that a million years have passed."

"The time dilation compensator will keep all our journeys in real Earth time. When you return, you will have been gone however many days you have spent out here, and no more."

"Good to know," said Colo. He glanced up at Tama. "So: separate rooms."

"Unless you are a couple. Are you a couple?"

He studied Tama's face. There was a question in her eyes, along with a bit of delight. He knew the answer was no, but he also knew that it was not a permanent no. But Tama was not like his other girls. If someday they were to be a couple, he would have to earn her . . . and she him.

"Our relationship is a work-in-progress," Colo replied.

"A wise answer."

"Very," said Tama.

The single word came from her in a husky, smoky tone, as if she had not expected such a response from him but was deeply pleased that he had made it. The tone gave Colo a little shiver of delight.

"Your quarters assignments stand. I will alert you when we arrive."

Colo stood up and turned around. The aft wall of the bridge was solid, without any sign of egress.

"Lettie said port side for me," said Tama. "But which side is that?"

"We'll have to learn ship terminology," said Colo. "But in baseball, the slang terms 'southpaw' and 'portsider' have the same meaning: a left-handed pitcher. So port must be on the left side of the ship."

Tama started in that direction, but Colo stopped her.

"Directions are determined by first facing the front of the ship, not the back," he told her. "That much, I do know. What I don't know is how to get out of here."

Tama studied the wall for a moment. Finally she said, "Lettie, display signs."

Two EXIT signs appeared above two doors in the wall.

"*Voilà*," said Tama.

ARTIFACT
by Rik Hunik

Sitting cross-legged in the basket, Darby watched the circle of blue sky overhead dwindle as the darkness pressed in against the feeble light of his battery-powered lantern. Dimly, about twelve feet away, a vertical rock wall surrounded him in a mathematically precise circle, so featureless he couldn't tell that he was descending, so perfect that it had to be artificial, which suggested he had found the right place, that his years-long gamble was about to pay off. The Artifact was deemed to be nothing more than a legend, but operating on the hypothesis that it actually existed had brought him here.

The thin cable connecting him to the surface disappeared into the dark, making it seem that he hovered unsupported and motionless, but he was sure he was descending at the same steady rate because he trusted his servants, reinforcing that trust with promises of large rewards. They didn't know why he was down here, they just knew that when he came back they would be very rich, and if he didn't come back he would gain his vengeance from beyond the grave.

So many of his colleagues were bogged down in endless analysis of this or that aspect of whatever minor ancient artifact they had, and while it was true that some breakthroughs, such as the cable he hung from, had benefited many and made a select few very rich, the odds were so low he didn't think he had a chance to win that lottery again.

Besides, his research had taught him that he didn't need to understand the technology or know how it worked in order to use it, so he concentrated on tracking down the Artifact, a legendary tool that allowed the wielder to accomplish nearly anything he could imagine.

Long ago the Artifact, created to bring peace during a long period of turmoil, had grown too powerful and became corrupted by evil in the hands of a rebel wizard who used it as an ultimate weapon, but before he could establish himself and consolidate his power he was defeated by a large coalition of wizards. The Artifact, too powerful to be destroyed, they cast into a bottomless pit which they created just for that purpose.

Darby didn't care about good or evil, he just wanted the power, so he gathered every reference to the Artifact, sifted through the mountains of material, distilled it and came up with several possible locations. Nobody else took the legends seriously, nobody thought the Artifact could be real, and everybody thought he was crazy to spend so much time and money searching for it. Sometimes he agreed with them, but he persisted, eliminating the possibilities one at a time until he found this hole.

Even though he owned a factory that produced the black fiber he had contracts to fulfill and could only take a fraction of a percent of the output for his personal use, so it had taken him several months to get together what he thought was enough, and then had come the nightmare of transporting the spools and heavy duty winch to the hole. He was certain his cable, thin at his end but growing thicker as it supported more weight, was strong enough, but as the minutes ticked by with no sign of a bottom he began to pray that his cable would be long enough.

He had only made two and three eighths miles of the cable, so when the two-mile call came down he broke into a nervous sweat despite the chill. He dropped another glowstone, watching it vanish into the depths, swallowed by the darkness like the others.

But no, this one was different. Far below, so dim he wasn't certain at first that it was really there, he saw a tiny spark, like a dim star in the night sky. His eyes glued to it, struggling to control his impatience, he watched the spark slowly grow brighter as the winch kept lowering him at the same steady rate.

Excitement grew as the light below resolved into a cluster of glowstones, all the ones he had dropped, and he called on the intercom to his servants above to slow the descent. His lust for power had brought him here but he tried not to get too excited because he was searching for a legend which might not exist, or may have been moved or destroyed, or might not work anymore, so even if this was the right place success was far from certain.

The basket thumped down on dry sand and he stepped out, turning up his lantern to see the wonders around him, but all there was to see was a circle of smooth sand, undisturbed except for the glowstones and his few footprints.

He pushed back the despair that threatened to take him. This had to be the place, the artifact had to be here somewhere.

He went around the entire perimeter, sliding his hand along the stone to feel any discrepancy that could indicate a door or an opening of some kind. When he came full circle to his own footprints he turned around and did the same thing in the opposite direction. This time he detected a barely discernable discrepancy and when he looked closely he saw a hole the size of a large pin. When he shone his light directly into it a door-sized section of the wall swung away, revealing another round chamber, this one only ten feet across.

There was nothing in the chamber except a small round platform of polished stone, almost like a pedestal, and sitting on the platform was a gleaming, golden cone three feet high, with a frosty, milky-white crystal set in the peak. He walked around it twice, and the second time around he saw some small, irregular impressions on opposite sides of the base of the cone. Moving closer he saw in the shifting reflections of his lantern that the impressions were hand-shaped, and he felt an immediate urge to fit his hands into those depressions.

He set the lantern on the sandy floor and reached with trembling hands for the cone, not knowing what to expect, but all he felt was cold metal. He shifted his hands slightly, felt something slip under his palms, and information flooded into his head. No, it was only a bit of information being fed into his head, but the method of communication was so intrusive it felt like a flood.

The upshot of the deal was that now he knew he needed light to activate the artifact. He turned up the lantern as bright as it would go and put his hands in the impressions again. This time the message was less intrusive and more informative; he needed more light, lots more light, as much as he could generate.

He went back to the other chamber, gathered all the surviving glowstones, and brought them back, then he went to the descent basket and got all the unused glowstones. He set them all up where he thought they'd be most effective, then activated them all to maximum brightness. At that level they would only last five or ten minutes but he prayed it would be enough.

Squinting against the intense light he touched the cone, felt information pour into his head, visions of what the artifact could do for him, the changes he could make, the power he would have, the amazing things he could do. He felt engines of ancient alien technology coming to life inside the cone, felt forces reaching out, accessing other dimensions, and he felt the power flowing into him, power such as he had never dreamed of possessing, power he could use to do anything he imagined.

Then it all slipped out of his grasp as the glowstones dimmed, their entire store of energy depleted seconds before the contacts could be completed, and he screamed out his anguish in a wordless curse to all the gods that ever were.

When he quit screaming to inhale he realized the only light in the pit was the glow of his lantern, and the thought of being stranded down here with no light at all jolted him back to sanity. He turned down the light to conserve the battery.

If he needed more light, he would get more light, even if he had to go all the way back to the Ten Cities to get it, though that was a last resort because it would increase the risk of discovery before he succeeded, which would probably result in his painful and prolonged death.

He climbed into the basket, activated the switch that connected his microphone to the speaker at the surface, and said, "Pull me up." They were his most loyal servants but he had not told them why he had come here, so there was no way for them to know he had failed, and no reason for him to tell them that.

Darby waited half a minute, then repeated the command. Still no response. Knowing his life would be in their hands during the descent he had brought his most trusted servants, and now he needed them to bring him back up because the artifact didn't work for him, but they were not answering.

With a thump a heavy object landed behind him, shattering part of his basket, and he jumped out just as another object crashed down right where he'd been standing. His guts clenched when he saw that it was the bodies of two of his servants, and while he wondered what had become of the others they dropped in to join the party, thumping down on the sand.

A bell chimed to indicate the communicator had been activated and an unknown voice with a peculiar accent said, "Did you really think the artifact was unguarded?"

The line went dead and before he had a chance to wonder who or what might have said that he heard the tension go out of the cable. Although incredibly light-weight for its amazing strength, a cable two miles long still weighed upwards of a thousand pounds, and if it landed on him he could easily be killed, injured or trapped.

The falling cable hissed as it piled higher and higher in the middle of the chamber, spreading toward the walls, leaving the artifact's chamber the only place for him to avoid getting crushed by them, and he had no sooner closed the door than the cable piled up against it, trapping him inside.

He sighed, leaned his back on the door and slid down to sit on the floor. What did it matter anyway? Without water he would be dead in a matter of days.

A shifting rustling noise came through the door and when he tried to open it he was surprised to discover that he could. The heap of cable sank slowly into the floor, getting noticeably smaller while he watched, the sand seeming to vibrate and reach up to grab the cable, to consume it, taking away any hope he had of recovering any food or water from the meager supply in his basket.

When the cable was gone a total silence descended and he noticed that his lamp was getting dimmer. Deep-seated despair washed through him, draining him of strength, and he slumped to the sand against the wall, so exhausted he fell asleep without even realizing. When he awoke the lantern was dark and cold.

Straining his eyes against the unrelenting darkness for what seemed like days but could have been less than an hour, he began to doubt that he would die of thirst before he went mad in the oppressive darkness.

A crack of light appeared across from him and to his amazement a door he hadn't suspected was there slid wide open, revealing a slim silhouette that could have been a man or a woman, but she revealed her sex when she spoke.

"You came for ultimate power, but that was denied you, and your servants paid the price. What of you? I can leave you here to suffer alone in the darkness, dying of thirst in four or five days, or I can offer you life."

Desperate though he was, Darby knew there had to be conditions to the offer, but he also knew in the pit of his stomach, that he would accept them, whatever they were, because there simply wasn't any other offer coming. "What kind of life?"

"You will get adequate food, comfortable quarters, a bit of leisure time, and you will not be worked beyond your endurance."

On close examination the offer was not very attractive; adequate food could be bland and unappealing, standards of comfort varied, a bit didn't sound like much, and just how close to his endurance would he be worked? "That sounds like slavery to me."

"Exactly. Now come. We have lots of work for you to do."

He climbed to his feet as fast as he could and broke into a clumsy run, desperately afraid she had only been teasing about giving him a choice, but the door waited, closing behind him.

Dragon Egg Soup
By S. Evan Townsend

The majordomo strode into the kitchen. Jack looked up, seeing the man filtered through the vapors of the cooking pots and the unruly black hair that hung over his face. The majordomo was tall, hawk-nosed, with quick grey eyes that were able to find the tiniest flaw in everything. He dressed, as usual, in a black suit, his posture rigid, and his bald pate uncovered.

"The king is dead," he announced in a loud voice.

Jack shrugged and returned to work plucking chickens. He was a simple chef's assistant, third class. His job consisted mainly of carrying half-prepared dishes from one point to another in the expansive kitchen at the rear of the castle. That, and plucking chickens, peeling potatoes, and cleaning the grease traps.

The king, the now-dead king, loved to eat and throw events and parties for his friends. It kept the kitchen busy.

The head chef pulled his tall, white hat from his head, removed his impeccable apron, and said, "I resign."

"Then you must appoint a successor," the majordomo snarled.

The head chef looked around, spotted Jack, and said, "Him."

The majordomo arched an eyebrow. "Him?"

"Yes, him."

"I see," the majordomo replied. Without a further word, he turned on a heel, and marched out of the room.

"And good luck, kid," the chef said, walking out of the back entrance to the kitchen.

Jack frowned and scratched his head. Was he now head chef? And why did the chef resign? He shrugged again, and returned to plucking chickens. It would work itself out, he knew. He wouldn't know how or why, as a simple assistant chef, third class. But he knew if he just kept up with his duties, all would be fine.

All the activity in the normally bustling kitchen had ceased. It was very quiet, except for the sound of Jack plucking chickens.

Then, he noticed all the other workers in the kitchen staring at him. And the look of pity in their eyes startled Jack. Was he in trouble? Did he do something wrong?

One of the pastry chefs, a rotund woman, clucked her tongue and said, "Such a waste; he's so young."

The majordomo returned and, as if refusing to enter the kitchen, stood in the arched doorway. He pointed at Jack. "You, come here." It was a demand that brooked no disobedience.

Jack dropped the half-plucked chicken he was holding and shuffled over, trying to stand straighter and look important. He felt the eyes of everyone in the room on him, especially the majordomo, who glared down at Jack.

"Yes, sir?" Jack asked. He had never talked to the majordomo. This was, for Jack, almost as daunting as he imagined talking to the king would be.

"What is your name?"

"Jack, sir."

"Any last name, Jack?"

"No, sir, just Jack. I never knew my ma and pa—"

"Never mind. First of all," the majordomo started, "cut that mop of hair."

"Yes, sir," Jack said automatically, but mourned inside for his hair. He liked it the way it was.

"You shall prepare," the majordomo continued, "the traditional coronation feast for the new king."

"But sir—" Jack tried but was stopped by the taller man.

"You will find recipes in the special events cookbook." He pointed to the bookshelf in the far corner of the kitchen. "The primary dish is dragon egg soup."

Jack only nodded. Then, he realized the majordomo said "book." "But I can't read, sir," Jack whined.

The majordomo rolled his eyes in an exaggerated movement. He pointed at a young assistant pastry chef. "You, girl, can you read?"

The girl blinked and looked over with wide eyes. She curtsied and said, "Yes, sir, my momma was very—"

"Fine. What is your name?"

"Molly, sir."

"Molly, you shall assist Chef Jack."

"Yes, sir." Molly curtsied again.

The majordomo leaned forward. "And do not fail me, Jack, or I shall have the head of the guards throw you in the dungeon." He looked at Molly. "Both of you in the dungeon."

Jack swallowed hard. "Wait. I don't want to be—"

"Then I suggest you get on your task, Head Chef Jack." Again the majordomo turned on his heel, and marched out of the doorway.

"I was going to say 'I don't want to be head chef,'" Jack muttered to himself. He stood there for a moment until someone touched his arm. He turned to see Molly looking at him expectantly. She was short and a bit plump with long, curly blonde hair. Her eyes were green as she smiled at him. "Come on," she said with what Jack thought was forced cheerfulness. "Let's see what this dragon egg soup is."

Jack nodded, and hoped "dragon egg soup" was only a name, like "devil's food cake" had nothing to do with the spawn of Hell. Or maybe a "dragon egg" was some exotic plant he'd never heard of.

Molly had to drag Jack to the shelf where the cookbooks where held. Jack reached for the largest one, but Molly pulled his hand away. "Not that one," she said. She pulled out one that was thin, yet leather-bound. The hide had been meticulously worked to make the cover very ornate. Jack wondered if the mysterious figures he assumed to be letters were real gold, as they shone in the light coming through the kitchen windows.

"This is the one," Molly announced. "'Recipes for Special Occasions,'" she intoned.

"What does it say about dragon egg soup?" Jack asked, trying to keep the anxiety from his voice but not quite succeeding.

"Just a moment." She didn't hide her exasperation.

Jack only nodded as Molly opened the book. The markings on the pages were a complete mystery to him. But Molly turned pages, found one, looked at it a moment, and then turned pages again.

"Here it is," she said triumphantly. "Dragon egg soup."

"How do I make it?" Jack asked, hoping against hope he'd be able to do so.

"Oh oh," Molly exclaimed.

"What?"

"The first ingredient: 'One fresh dragon egg.'"

Jack frowned. "Where do I get a dragon egg?" He looked around the room, and realized everyone was watching him.

"From a dragon's lair, you twit," a voice cackled out.

Jack looked for the source of the sound, and found a crinkled old man, bent over a gnarled cane, glaring at him.

"What did you say?" Jack asked.

The man took halting steps forward as if every movement hurt. "From a dragon's lair. Where else?"

"And who are you?" Molly asked. Jack wished he had thought of that.

The man laughed with that cackling voice. "Never mind me. You'd best be on your way to get a dragon egg unless you want to be thrown in the dungeon."

"Where do I find a dragon's lair?" Jack asked, his stomach churning.

"High in the Great Mountains. That's where there be dragons."

"Dragons are a myth," Molly said, standing straighter and talking louder. "I've read books and—"

The stooped, old man guffawed. "I'm older than your books, little girl. I know what was never written."

Jack and Molly just looked at each other.

"Climb as high as you can, until you can climb no more, and that's where you'll find dragons," the old man continued.

Jack shook his head.

"Best you be going," the old man said. "The coronation will be in the morning."

"I'll go with you," Molly said. "Maybe I can help."

Jack thought about it. The dungeon didn't seem so bad compared to the task before him. No one had seen a dragon. No one knew what they would do. And how was he to climb the snowy and craggy Great Mountains?

"I won't do it," he said defiantly. "The majordomo can throw me in the dungeon."

"But he'll throw me in there, too," Molly cried. "We have to do this. It's not up to you. Both our lives are in peril." Life expectancy in the dungeon was approximately three months.

Jack gazed at Molly. If it were his own life, he wouldn't care. But it was also this girl's life. And, that, he wouldn't be responsible for ending. He set a determined look on his face. "Fine, we'll do it."

Molly put the book back on the shelf.

Jack walked toward the back door exit of the kitchen. Finding the Great Mountains would be no problem: they loomed over the kingdom.

"Sir?" someone asked.

Jack ignored them, knowing they couldn't be talking to him.

"Jack, sir?" they said again.

He turned. "Yes?" He wondered why they were calling him "sir."

"Sir," the man said, who had been the assistant chef. "What do you wish for us to do in the meantime?"

Jack thought a moment. "Prepare the other dishes for the coronation. Do what you normally do. And find someone to pluck those chickens." He pointed to the hens he'd been working on.

"Yes, sir," the man said. He didn't hide his disdain for Jack.

Jack didn't have the energy to care. He figured he'd either die getting the dragon egg or die in the dungeon. Then he had an idea.

"Why don't you go find a dragon egg?" he said to the assistant chef.

"You don't want me to do that," the man replied. "You need me to prepare all the other dishes so you're not thrown in the dungeon."

Jack thought a moment, and decided that was probably the best thing to do. If he had a chance of not dying, it was to make sure everything was perfect if he did managed to return with a dragon egg.

"Yes," he whispered and walked out, Molly following him.

"I don't understand," Molly said. "I've never heard of the king having an heir. There's no prince or princess. Who are they going to coronate?"

Jack shrugged. "I don't really care." He was sure whatever happened, he would, if he survived, go on through life as miserable and worthless as before. He slept on straw under a lean-to of discarded wood. He ate kitchen scraps and food deemed not suitable for human consumption.

The castle's rear courtyard filled with activity as Jack had never seen it before. Must have to do with the King's death and the pending coronation, he decided. But, he ignored it all and walked in a morose shuffle toward the gate. Even here he could see the snow-covered peaks of the Great Mountains.

"Should we stop at the bladesmith?" Molly asked, affecting a light tone.

Jack shook his head. "No, if I have to fight a dragon, I will die. And all I need is for a sword to clank at the wrong moment."

Molly nodded, but Jack could tell she was deep in thought. "There might be other dangers along the way."

Jack stopped and thought. "Yes, perhaps you are right." They turned toward the armory.

"Do you know how to use a sword, young man?" the bladesmith asked, locking his black eyes on Jack.

Jack shook his head.

"Likely as not cut your own arm off without training."

"Can you train him?" Molly asked.

"Do you have a couple of years to spare?" The man spat on the ground. "And I'm not the man to do it, anyway."

"Who is?" Jack asked, dreading the answer.

"The Sergeant of the Guards," the bladesmith responded. "But he's much too busy to deal with the likes of you. Lots of dignitaries coming to the castle for the funeral and coronation that he has to keep safe."

Jack frowned. "Thank you." He left the armory. Looming above was the Great Mountains, still, as if they were mocking him.

"Guess I'd better go," he said as Molly stood beside him.

"*We'd* better go," she said. "I'm going to help."

"No," Jack snapped. "It's too dangerous."

"What, for a girl?" She curled the last word into a contemptuous tone.

"For anyone. No need to get us both killed."

"I can help," Molly said. "You have no idea how big a dragon egg is. You might need two people to carry it."

Jack tried not to roll his eyes. He knew Molly was trying to be helpful,l but he didn't know why she insisted on coming on this probably fatal quest.

"Suit yourself," he finally said, giving her an out, he thought.

"Let's get some water and food," she said, taking his hand and pulling him toward the storehouse. This is where the guards kept their provisions, Jack knew.

Inside it was dim and dank, but Molly grabbed two skins full of water and a bag of dried food that was supposed to last a soldier at least a day. Then, she snagged a second one, put it all in a backpack she found, and handed it to Jack.

He slipped it on and made an "oof" sound as it bent his back with its weight. He couldn't imagine carrying this up the slopes of the Great Mountains. But what choice did he have?

Finally, they left the castle through the rear gate. Two guards stood there, their armor reflecting the sunlight. They didn't say a word as Jack and Molly passed.

Jack turned west, toward the Great Mountains. At first, it was almost like a pleasant summer walk through the kingdom. The road was broad and well-maintained without ruts or muddy spots. Green fields demarked the edge of the lane, and farmers were working with their animals or their crops. Some would wave and, surprised, Jack would wave back.

"No one seems very sad the king is dead," Jack said.

"Lives go on, I guess," Molly replied.

Too quickly, the road stopped being wide and flat and became narrow, curvy, and climbed up the side of a mountain.

"How do we get an egg from a dragon?" Jack breathed hard as the road had turned to a trail, and the trail turned steep.

"Has anyone ever seen a dragon?" Molly asked. "We don't know how big they are."

"Legend says they are huge," Jack said. "Big as a house."

"Can you trust legend?"

Jack shrugged. "I don't know."

They trudged in silence, Jack leading the way. Molly had no

trouble keeping up and, in fact, Jack thought perhaps he was moving slower than she wished.

The temperature dropped as they went highe,r and Jack wished he'd brought warmer clothes. He berated himself for not realizing this as the Great Mountains were crowned by snow.

The trail nearly disappeared. Jack knew the only way to go was up, higher and higher. Molly matched him stride for stride as the wind flayed their clothes and twisted their hair. Jack hugged himself and looked up at the peaks above him. How far did he have to climb to reach the dragons? He thought many times about giving up but the idea of the dungeon, and being responsible for Molly going there, sustained his strength.

The patches of snow appeared before they found a dragon, and deepened and grew the higher they went until they labored through knee deep whiteness.

Jack stopped and looked back at the valley. The castle appeared the size of a penny, something Jack had seen but never possessed. The green fields surrounding looked like a patchwork quilt. He was very high in the Great Mountains. The sun was low on the horizon and Jack knew it would get colder if night fell.

Jack and Molly shared some water and food from their supplies, hurrying lest it get too dark. They left the heavy backpack there, resolving to recover it on the way back down.

Without warning, Jack felt heat from ahead. He saw an orange glow against the snow-covered cliffs. He grabbed Molly, and pulled her behind a rock.

"What?" she asked.

"I think a dragon is close." Jack whispered, hoping not to draw the attention of the beast.

Molly's eyes went wide, and she nodded.

"Listen," Jack said, still whispering, "I'll draw it away, you go into its lair and get an egg."

"Draw it away how?"

Jack shrugged. "I don't know."

"What's its lair?"

"I assume a cave, or something."

Molly rolled her eyes.

"Just look for eggs," Jack hissed. "Ready?"

Molly took a deep breath and nodded.

"Go!" Jack barked. He ran for the heat and the light. There was little snow here, likely because of the warmth of the beast. Creeping around a boulder, he saw the dragon. It was as long as one of the castle towers was tall. Its head was the size of a wagon, and most of that was a toothy mouth. Bat-like wings folded against its thin, scaly body. Its eyes were closed and it was breathed softly. Each exhalation shot out twin jets of orange flame through its nostrils. Jack's skin broke out in sweat when this happened.

The dragon's tail extended to be just inside a black cave. The opening looked like a dark mouth with a row of teeth-like icicles hanging from the tip. Jack could see Molly walking slowly and quietly, trying to sneak into the opening past the tail.

Jack thought for a minute that if the thing stayed asleep, they might get away with this.

Then Molly accidentally stepped on a downed icicle, and it cracked in two with a sound that seemed to echo across the mountains.

Melon-sized eyes burst open, and the dragon raised its head high over Jack. It turned to look toward the source of the sound, but Molly had managed to hide inside the cave.

Jack worried the dragon would go inside and find her. He picked up a rock and threw it at the head. "Hey, you, worm, you big ugly lizard," he yelled.

The dragon apparently forgot the cave, and turned to look at Jack, its slit pupils narrowing.

"Yeah, you, filthy monster. Come get me." And Jack turned and ran, knowing the dragon could blast him with fire at any moment. He jumped behind a large boulder just as the worm spat flame. The heat was intense, even as the rock protected Jack. He tried not to scream, but the fire was too hot. Scalding water ran down his back, and he realized it was snow that hand melted from atop the stone.

When the conflagration ended, he hoped the dragon had to take in a breath giving him time to escape. He ran down the mountain, away from the cave, trusting the dragon would follow and allow Molly to get an egg. He hit deep snow and that slowed him down. Fear and momentum kept him going.

He looked back and, sure enough, the dragon undulated down the slope.

Jack tripped over something. He stumbled and rolled, thinking now he was dead as the dragon would surely catch him. But what he'd tripped over was the bones and armor of a man, half-buried in the snow. He picked up the man's steel shield. It was almost as big as Jack, rusting along the edges, and icy cold to the touch. Jack held it over his body as, again, the monster blasted him with fire. The heat this time was even worse than before, and Jack yelled. His hand holding the shield burned as the steel heated.

Jack dropped the shield and sprinted away. He saw a sword, but from the size of it decided its weight would only slow him down.

He heard air whooshing and turned to see the dragon, wings extended, flying behind him. He jumped down a short ledge, snow softening his landing, and plastered himself against the cliff. The dragon flew over him, but turned in the sky and hovered, its wings blasting down a hurricane that almost knocked Jack over. He could swear it was smiling as it opened it mouth to shoot fire.

Jack jumped down again. This was a longer fall and he hit hard, knocking the breath out of him. There was less snow here to cushion his fall, and he hurt his leg. He rolled onto his back to see the belly of the dragon as it blasted flame at the ledge where he had been.

Jack stood and tried to run, but his leg hurt too badly. He knew he couldn't escape that way.

He limped off, found a nook between two rocks, and slid into it, crouching low. There was drifted snow in the crevasse and he put his burned hand in it and sighed with relief.

The dragon flew past him.

A few moments later, it came back, hovering over the mountainside. It blasted fire randomly against the rocks in apparent rage and frustration. Or, maybe, Jack thought, to drive him out of hiding.

Without warning, the beast turned in the air, screamed a screech that made Jack cover his ears, and flew back up the mountain. Jack hoped Molly had gotten a dragon egg and escaped.

He waited what felt like hours. The sun was very low but it was still light enough to see. Eventually Molly walked by. He called out to her.

She jumped and squinted to see him in the dark cranny.

"Jack?"

"Yes. Where's the dragon?"

"It went back to its lair. I thought it had killed you. I barely got out before it got back."

"It must have given up on finding me," Jack said.

"Well, I can barely see you so, yes, it must not have found you."

Jack came out of the cranny, his leg still hurting and his hand throbbing with searing pain. Molly was empty handed. "You didn't get an egg?" Jack whined, thinking they were going to have to go back again to get a dragon egg.

"There were none."

"Then how are we supposed to make dragon egg soup?" Jack cried.

"I have an idea." Molly grinned.

*

The majordomo tasted the soup. He spent a few moments rolling it around his mouth. Then, setting down the spoon, he said, "Needs a touch more salt."

Jack nodded. "Yes, sir."

"And you shall serve it personally, Jack," the majordomo ordered.

"Y-yes, sir," Jack replied.

The majordomo pivoted on his heel and stepped out of the kitchen.

Jack almost fainted.

"I told you it would work," Molly whispered. "No one has had dragon egg soup since the last coronation fifty years ago. Even if they had it then, they probably don't remember what it tastes like."

Jack smiled and nodded.

"Now let's get you cleaned up." She grinned and ran her fingers through his mop of hair.

Jack, dressed in the Head Chef's finest uniform, his hair cut neatly, pushed the cart into the great dining chamber with the pot of "dragon egg soup" on top. His right hand was bandaged where it had been burned holding the shield, and his leg still hurt, causing him to limp.

The majordomo and one other man were the only ones there. Jack frowned. He thought this was a celebration. And where was the new king? And the other man was old, crinkled, and leaning on a cane. Jack realized it was the old man from the kitchen that told him how to find the dragon eggs. Except his cane was now straight and glossy and he was dressed in red robes with a tall red hat. Even Jack recognized it as the garb of the cardinal.

Molly stood behind Jack, carrying the ceremonial ladle to help serve.

"Long live the king!" the cardinal cried.

"Hail the king!" the majordomo called out.

"King?" Jack asked. "We are the only ones here. Who is the king?"

The cardinal smiled, which wrinkled up his face even more. "Dear boy, you don't know who your parents were, do you?"

"No, sir," Jack replied. "I'm an orphan."

"You are not," the cardinal declared. "You are heir to the throne."

"Me?"

"Yes," the majordomo said, his voice respectful for the first time in Jack's memory. "We have a tradition in this kingdom. The crown prince or princess is not raised as royalty. They are sent among the common people to learn what it is like to be a peasant. Then, they must pass a trial to become king. Your trial was dragon egg soup."

Jack suddenly felt guilty. "Then I failed. For it is not dragon egg soup. We used chicken eggs."

The cardinal smiled softly. "Yes, we know. There's no such thing as dragon eggs. We don't know how dragons reproduce. Or perhaps they are immortal. But they are definitely not oviparous."

Jack had no idea what that word meant.

"But," the cardinal continued, "you have proven yourself worthy to be king. You are smart: you figured out how to make 'dragon egg soup' without dragon eggs. You are brave because you faced the dragon. You are tough as you climbed the mountains to get to the dragon, and climbed back down with a hurt leg. You are persistent because you never gave up trying to get the dragon eggs. And you care about others because you worked to keep Molly out of the dungeon and risked your life to keep her safe from the dragon."

Jack shook his head. It was too much to believe. He was the king? "And what if I failed?"

"Then your younger brother or sister would be tested, next. But you didn't fail, Jack. You are the king."

Just then, a crowd came in the room crying "Long live the king!" as Jack was led to the throne. A crown was placed on his head and he was handed a scepter. He held it in his bandaged hand despite the pain.

Molly stood by the pot of chicken egg soup, looking confused.

The mass of people, all dressed in finery Jack had only dreamed of, sat at the table as the rest of the kitchen staff came in and started serving the coronation banquet. Jack noticed the head chef, who had resigned, was among them.

"You'll need to select advisors," the cardinal was saying.

"Advisors?"

"Yes, people to help you make the correct decisions. I have some ideas: the most learned men and women of the kingdom."

Jack smiled and pointed at Molly. "Then I choose her, first."

Molly looked at Jack with confusion in her eyes. "Me?"

"Yes, you. And you can start by teaching me to read."

"Start?" Molly asked.

"Well, eventually I will probably need to choose a queen, too."

Molly grinned big, and came to stand by the throne.

Exile by Choice
By Kate Runnels

The round trip journey of some 8.44 ly and then the exploration of Alpha Centauri had been long, grueling, satisfying and wonderful for Kith and the twenty-one others returning. But they were leaving some behind. Twenty-five had departed Mars. One had never arrived and the three others had died in natural unforeseen occurrences. One drowned and two were taken in a rock slide. It had happened a while ago, and Kith had worked through her sorrow at the loss, but for those of the family's waiting for those four it would be fresh when they found out their loved ones would never be returning.

The exploration team had spent an entire year, a full Earth year, exploring the Alpha Centauri system and the one habitable planet therein. They had taken to calling the planet itself just, Alpha. In that year a lot had happened, but the strongest and most important to Kith and the others in the corps, was that it would sustain human life. And now they were returning home to share that knowledge and the success of Dr. Nagano's project for human colonization.

Four years and thirty-seven days out, a full earth year on Alpha and four years thirty-seven days returning.

A total of nine years and seventy-four days and Kith and the team were due to arrive on Mars within minutes. The same place they had started, the same laboratory, and hopefully the same people. But even though it had only been a year for them, in actual time, it had been nearly nine for the others. Nine years was a long time, even when most of the human population lived, with help, into their early hundreds.

The team was within the Sol system and had passed by Saturn and the particles that made up the rings. To Kith they smelled of strawberries. The synesthesia that came with this mode of travel was something she had never told anyone else, lest they think her unstable from traveling in this truly experimental way. She didn't know if they others experienced this as well. They would not see Jupiter this time through as they had on their way out, which was fine with her, as Jupiter felt heavy on her brain as a weight pressing down.

Twenty eight minutes and they would have returned from one of the most fateful missions for all mankind. Like Rider, Perrault, Chan and Arshavin arriving on Mars; or Armstrong and Aldrin on the moon. Gagarin, Yeager, Lewis and Clark, the names of all those explorers trailing back through history to appear at pivotal moments.

On this trip, Kith had seen and done something only twenty-five others could say they'd done. And they had proven humans could exist outside the Sol system.

The home team had known of their arrival time since they had left, she and the others all hoped their families would be there waiting for them. Kith especially; she and her family hadn't parted on the best of terms. Nine years was a long time. Sadness crept into her happiness at a great mission and their homecoming. And Alex had left her long before she had ever left for Alpha.

The entire expedition, what she'd seen and helped explore and create and be a part of, yeah, it had been worth it, but the loss of someone close to her still hurt. It hadn't been that long for her.

She and the others would only have aged physically a year. Everyone that had stayed on Mars and Earth would be nine years older. Her father would be seventy-three and her mother seventy-two. Her younger brother would be older than her now.

Kith shoved those thoughts aside as they approached Mars. They zipped down to the red planet, that glowed a brilliant orange to her eyes, and the differences in the domed colonies couldn't set into her mind before they were into Dr. Nagano's lab and rematerialized within.

It was only the third time she had experienced this, with some of the others. Most of the expedition was experiencing it for the second time. It was still a strange sensation, as she was light one moment and then she was solid and back into her mortal form, standing on a planet and being affected by gravity and subject to sounds and light and human sensations again.

There was a reception committee waiting for them and their ears were assaulted by cheers and clapping. Champaign was shoved into their hands before they could recover. But soon they were ushered into medical after the cheers died down. She and all the rest of the team understood the necessity but she didn't have to like it, and noticed none of the others felt comfortable going through medical to be checked out for health. Each one knew they were healthy.

At least they didn't have to be debriefed. Their observations and the exploration team records had been recorded onto memory chips and handed over on their arrival. This passed on their responsibility. Those others would start the next stage of full colonization.

Medical through with them, pronouncing them healthy, which they grumbled under their breath at the doctors, they had known that. Now they could finally meet with their friends and family flown to Mars for the reception. This was an historic moment for mankind.

Kith wasn't the last out of processing, but close to it. She bounced onto the tips of her toes to see over and around the milling bodies of her friends, the other explorers with their families and loved ones.

The murmur of voices filled the reception room, and Kith spotted several cameras recording the event, but no reporters thankfully; at least not yet. She popped back up onto her toes again, and finally spotted her brothers.

She pushed her way through the milling bodies of the others to her brothers, a little saddened that it was only her brothers. But before she knew it, she was crying and hugging them, and feeling them hug her back. She pulled back finally, wiping her eyes, all with a smile. But she had to ask, "Mom? Dad?"

"They are fine," Kristian assured Kith, "But they couldn't take the strain of leaving Earth."

Kith nodded in understanding. Dr. Nagano's method of traveling was still new and unknown. If they hadn't returned it would not have been accepted, but it should take hold with their successful return.

Kazimir, Kith's younger brother, stood tall beside her, almost as tall as Kristian. "You've grown a beard, Kaz. It looks good on you."

He smiled at the compliment and she took the time to glance around the large reception room again. They both seemed to guess her intent. "Alex isn't coming," said Kaz. "I checked for you. It was a forceful no."

That hurt.

Though, she had known, even anticipated it.

She felt a nudge on her shoulder and turned to the bearded face of her younger brother, although he was older than she was now. "Come on Sis, you must tell us all about your grand voyage to another star."

"And you'll visit mom and dad, I trust?" that was her older brother, Kristian, still acting like an older brother.

"Of course I will. Before I head to Earth though, I'll need to find out when the next mission is scheduled and for where. But I'm sure we are all due a month of vacation, at least."

Her two brothers grew silent in the forest of families. Kith glanced from face to face. "This was only the beginning. With viable colonization, it opens up enormous possibilities. Or has the population diminished in the time we've been gone?"

"No, but mom and dad won't like you going back out there," said Kaz.

"They didn't like me going in the first place," she said. "It's my right. I worked long and hard to get here. Human kind can be saved with this." She hated the fact she had to defend herself again as she had last year to her, and nine years earlier to them.

She sighed. "I can't explain what it's like to you, to travel in such a manner."

Kristian too sighed. "Well, then explain what Alpha was like."

Kith grinned, forcing cheerfulness. This was supposed to be a party, a homecoming, but she couldn't wait to go back out and explore the vastness of her galaxy. "Alpha, being a binary system, there are days when it was never dark. Then there were days it never got light. We stayed indoors then, stayed in the camp. The predators came at night. Flying mammals, the size of horses, looked about like flying squirrels and they hunted in packs."

"What did they hunt?"

"The nocturnal, well, giant lemurs. Hairless, eyeless, with migratory habits, like lemurs. The name kinda stuck."

She told tales and they regaled her with stories of their own lives as well, and for a time, Kith pretended everything was fine in her world. That the confrontation with her parents wasn't coming, hiding the fact she longed to head back out into the black, doing something she understood, for a cause she was passionate about.

"No, mom, I'm not staying on earth; or Mars, or the outlying colonies! There are no opportunities for me here, besides the fact, I trained for this and was hand selected by Dr. Nagano and his team. Not to mention my professor, Dr. Callaxon, is heading up those teams. Furthermore, I can't fathom not returning. There are some of the most amazing things out there, just waiting to be experienced."

"Name one," challenged her mother, sitting back in her chair, with arms crossed and glaring at Kith, like she had always done. Kith had always been a disappointment to her mother. She glanced at her father, but he was ignoring the argument, like he usually did, watching a match between River and Velez.

Kith matched her mother's glare, but then her eyes softened with the memory. "I skipped through the rings of Saturn, mother. I felt the gravity pull on my senses, the ice in the rings tingled and smelled of sunshine after the rain. That is only one. There is some much more."

Her mother snorted.

"Words, just words."

"Not to me and the others who have experienced this. It goes beyond words, mother, you would know that if you opened your mind."

*

Her homecoming was not going well. Last night had been wonderful, with a lovely home cooked dinner, but this morning they'd asked what she planned to do now that she was back.

"It had already taken nine years away from us. How can you be so selfish and even think about leaving us again? How many years will you be away then?"

"How can you be so selfish and ask me to stay? I have found something I truly believe in, and you would ask me to give that all up?"

Her father turned his gaze from the match to the two women. Kith noticed and stopped him before he began. "Don't bother, Markis. Our minds are already made up. I'm going for a walk."

She went out the walled courtyard from their family room,

locking the gate behind her. Buenos Aires hadn't changed much in the nine years she'd been gone. There were still people worse off than others and willing to take what those others had. Her parents had fled Prague to live in South America, during the Religion War that encompassed the Middle East, western and Eastern Europe and parts of Asia and Russia. That was long before even her older brother had been born though. This had been the only house she'd known when growing up.

Dressed once again in her old clothes nine years out of date, Kith blended in with the population. She stepped over the dog crap, near but not next to a tree, and kept walking. The streets hadn't been repaired since they'd first been laid down, so as she went, she stepped from old pavement to cobblestones, both broken with age. Cars passed going where their drivers took them. Off in the distance she even saw a buggy drawn by a single horse.

She passed a corner café with the tele screens showing the match on one, with another showing their already famous return to Doctor Nagano's lab on mars. She walked on past. It was unlikely she would be recognized, but she preferred anonymity.

Kith finally slowed in her escape from her parent's house, many blocks away at a different café and decided to sit and get something to eat and drink. She had just ordered and the waitress left when she heard the conversation from the group behind her.

"Have you heard about the lottery?"

"No, what?"

"They are going to put everyone's name in to see who gets drawn. Those who are will be shipped off to Alpha Centauri. It's forced colonization. The new U.N. will draw lots by country to relieve the overcrowding. The most populous first, I've heard. Argentina isn't first, but within the first fifteen."

"They can't just ship us off, can they? And all because we took in refugees? That's not right."

"Just you watch and see. They will."

Kith frowned, not having heard of this, as the gossipers paid for their drinks and left. She stayed longer than she had intended, as the café had a tele screen running the news. She waited through sports until they played exactly what the gossiper had been talking about. The U.N. was going to utilize Dr. Nagano's incredible feat of science to force colonization. Kith hated that. She had hoped enough people would want to colonize on their own. Some would, she knew, but to force others. She waited through the entire piece, and then left.

She forced herself to try and be civil to her mother and father, wanting to spend as much time with her family as possible before returning to the newly formed Exploration Corps, as sub branch of the new colonization minister of Dr. Nagano. Even now, new explorers were applying and going through initial examinations to be sent out to new worlds and new systems. While others were being rounded up and sent to mars, prior to colonizing Alpha.

The city took on a different feel over the weeks, as country after country went through their lottery. Argentina's was soon approaching. The people were edgier, angrier, and many spent their free time milling about shops and café's which constantly ran updates on the lottery for Alpha.

Kith tried to stay as inconspicuous as possible, not wanting to be singled out, now because her name was tied to the program and Dr. Nagano. Instead of being a hero, she was being vilified for working with the government. But she herself had nothing to do with the lottery.

Kith passed the milling crowd on the corner; their voices growing louder to be heard. Kith sensed the violence lurking just below the surface ready to strike when the time was right. She'd once seen a crocodile do the exact same thing during one of her extreme survivalist training trips. It sank slowly down, with barely a ripple in the water. Kith watched it go scanning the bank for its intended prey. Kith had waited. The croc had waited. If Kith hadn't known it was about to strike, she would have missed it. It had happened quickly. So too, could this.

She slowed to watch the angry crowd as she passed. They were getting closer and closer to that striking point. She'd been in one futball riot when she was younger and that was enough for her. As she watched, a bus pulled up and more people boiled out to join the first.

She spun forward, sensing she was about to run into someone. And then stopped in shock; this was the last person she had expected to see here. "Alex."

It was the one person she had longed to see upon her return and knew she never would. But now, there she stood, so beautiful still, looking confused down at Kith. Her expression changed as recognition sank in. her face turned from shock to anger.

The slap came as a surprise.

Kith felt the sting and heard the words at the same time. "Damn you, Kith Korvo!"

Kith blocked the second slap before it connected. "You left me, Alexia! You left me and the program. It was your decision."

"Only because you were already leaving. You were leaving my life and seemed so happy about doing it."

"Not happy about leaving you," Kith whispered.

"But you still did, didn't you."

"And I would do it again. I'm not going to lie to you. I'm not going to lie to you Alexia, I still love you. For me, it's only been a year."

Kith saw Alexia's eyes focus behind Kith, and it was then the noise intruded. The crowd had reached their point and had stuck. The crowd had gone from loud noises, to loud noises and riotous mob. They surged down the street at the two of them. Others had already backed into doorways to stay out of the way.

The front rank glared at the two of them, mostly men, and Argentina still was mostly anti-gay, filled and fueled by the refuge Muslim community. The hate filled eyes glared at the two of them. Kith's eye flicked to the knives and hockey sticks held in many hands.

Kith grabbed hold of Alex's hand and yanked her back against the wall. "What is going on in this city?"

"That precious trip of yours and the lotteries."

"I have had no part in the lotteries!"

Then the mob was abreast of them and flowing around them. They had to go with the crowd, even backed up against the wall, they were forced off; they had to go with or be trampled. Kith was pressed in by bodies all around. The noise drowned out even Alex beside her, who gripped her hand as if it were a life line. Kith kept the same hold on Alex. Kith's eyes darted around, looking for a way out. She tried to slow them, but they were pushed from behind and she almost went to her knees. She smelled the sweat of too many bodies.

The buildings loomed too large around them, their gray concrete seeming ominous, and more so, when it started bouncing the policia lights off their façade. That was the only tell they had to the policia's involvement. They couldn't hear the sirens, and with their arrival, the press of bodies increased.

Kith's grip began to loosen on Alex's from fear sweat from the two of them. Tear gas floated to them. And they started coughing slightly. Those in the front pressed back and those in the back not knowing what was happening to the front pushed forward. Kith and Alex were stuck in the middle.

Along with tear gas, the policia sent out smoke screen, the rioters had started fires, and the buildings and the people were obscured. Her eyes stung and watered. Kith couldn't see more than fifteen feet beyond. She felt snot dripping from her nose because of the tear gas, and that tickle in her throat worsened. She began pushing Alex to the side to get out of the crush. The two sides were ebbing and flowing, people running, and Kith wondered when the shooting would begin.

Pushing and shoving intensified, and Kith gripped harder to Alex, but it was to no use. Someone from the crowd pushed their way between the two and Kith lost her. The sweaty palms disengaged. Quickly, Kith spun, but her eyes were watering and the smoke was so thick it took a moment to locate Alex. Now on the ground, near the curb. She was struggling to stand. Kith watched in horror, knowing she wasn't close enough to help, when a nameless someone ran full tilt into Alex. The man's knee connected with Alex's head.

Kith raced over. Alex was unconscious. She scooped the slighter though taller women into her arms and backed into an angle of two buildings. This had gotten too far out of hand, far too quickly.

It seemed like hours, but it must have been only fifteen minutes when the crowd dispersed, the policia were clearing the area and the smoke and gas cleared around the same time. One policia officer saw her then, intending to arrest the two of them. It was only then Kith used her clout as a returning explorer, and as one of the first eight. She pushed and bullied and had them rush Alex to the nearest hospital, giving the officer with them her statement at the same time.

Once she saw Alex was getting the care she needed, Kith relaxed a little. It was then she realized that Alex had a family. The hospital had called them in once Kith had left her side. She had a wife and son sitting by her bedside when Kith returned. She stopped at the door jam. The wife looked up, questioningly.

"Are you the one who brought my Alex in?"

Kith swallowed and then nodded, afraid to say anything.

"Oh, thank you. Thank you so much."

"I, uh, I just wanted to make sure she was alright. Now you're here, I'll be going." Kith nodded and left. Knowing she was fleeing, like she had fled her parent's house and not caring. The officer assigned to her, guided her out the hospital saying something about the chief wanting to speak with her.

Kith only nodded. Drained. Too much had happened today and she was drained of feeling. While in with the chief of policia, an aide interrupted them. An aide from the president sent to invite Kith to meet him in the casa rosada.

The same officer dropped her off at her parent's house much later that night. Kith was numb and had no idea what she was to do at the president's house tomorrow. Her parents greeted her with hugs and warmth and Kith fell to sleep and dreamed of space.

She dutifully went to the banquet, she found out it was in her honor, and the president pinned a medal on her for being the only Argentino on the first trip to Alpha as an explorer. Kith smiled duly and shook hands and said very little, the world had changed so much in nine years and all the politics from nine years ago had no bearing on now.

She knew she was being used to make the lottery forced on other Argentinos to seem tolerable and she hated it. She called for volunteers, going into detail how open and wonderful it was, without skimping on the danger.

But she knew, in all her heart that Dr. Nagano's work, his incredible feat of science and technology that allowed travel at the speed of light, would save humanity. So Kith persevered. If she could leave the world she loved for nine years and planned on longer trips, then so could other adventurers, she told the press.

"And being transformed and to travel at the speed of light... it's like nothing else on this world." They laughed at her joke.

Her time on Earth fast approached its end and Kith couldn't wait. The strain with her parents and brothers was telling. As was dealing with the press and the lottery and the blowback from the riot. She longed for Mars and clean space. She would leave for mars the next day. Not by SMT but by conventional fission means.

Once again, she found herself locking the gate leading out of her parents place. She would be leaving here with mixed emotions. She loved her parents and brothers, and her brothers families, but after nine years, they had changed and she might never see her parents again. But this had always been her dream, to travel through space. To work in space.

She squared her shoulders, she had to make one last stop before leaving it all behind.

Her knuckles rapped on the door.

A moment later Alex answered, stepping out and closing the door behind her, instead of inviting Kith in. She had suffered a concussion and a few mild lacerations from the riot.

"I hated you," she started off. "I hated you so much for leaving." Alex took in a deep breath and her tone softened. "But I got over it, and I have a wonderful family."

"I saw that," Kith said. "I'll miss you."

Alex surprised her and gripped her in a crushing emotional hug. "And I still love you, too. Now go before I start to cry."

It was too late for Kith.

Back on Mars in the exploration corps headquarters, she smiled at the twenty other explorers who had gone to Alpha and had decided to return like her, for more exploration of other worlds. There were others too, new explorers, just as eager as they had been that first time.

This was where Kith belonged. They were all exiles by choice.

Fire and Snow
By Priya Sridhar

This tale starts with dancing and a witch. The witch, Isolde of the East Wind, was my mother's cousin and my aunt. She is my namesake, as is the winter in which I was born. My name is Isolde, and my brother is Blaise; we haven't heard those names in years, however. Most call us Snowdrop and Firedrake, or by our surname Perrault.

Mother could not have children, even though she married young and was in the prime of health. Instead of waiting for her time to come, she implored Aunt Isolde to grant her children. Witches never do anything for free, however, and Aunt Isolde was no different.

When the winter solstice approached, she wrapped my mother in a fur cloak, brought her to a clearing in the middle of the woods, and introduced her to Old Man Winter. They had a nice waltz, and Old Man Winter complimented her gentle feet. At the end of the night he gave her an ice cube to swallow, a cube that glowed gentle green. It slid down her throat easily and made her shiver. During the next summer solstice, Aunt Isolde enveloped Mother in a summer dress made of powdery butterfly wings and wheat sheaves before presenting her to the Summer King. He danced with her also and taught her how to leap across the great desert bonfires. One flame snagged on her gown and curled around her. She didn't burn, although the heat made her tingle and traveled down her throat. Her body was on fire, but the flames left no mark on her skin or skirts. She didn't even bear a burn on her lip.

Mother still has the dress; I studied it from time to time, before tucking it away in her small trunk, because the gleaming, shimmering scales make me weep.

We are twins because we were born at the same time, on September 20th during the year of King Reginald. We couldn't have been more opposite, however; Firedrake had red hair, and bushy eyebrows, and I had white-blond hair and lashes as fair and faint as frozen mist. He spent most of our summers sprinting through the blazing wildfires, laughing as the flames parted around him, while I took to the cellar during the hot months. My time came during the winter, where my bare feet made the ground glaze with frost. Where I danced, snow crystals bloomed beneath my long toes.

Father, while he enjoyed watching us dance, often frowned if we had not done useful work for the day. He apprenticed Firedrake to a baker in the nearby village, where Firedrake could handle the choking ovens. As for me, he had me assist the ice harvesters from the mountains, and I learned how to entertain the men with folksongs and common dances. Father never had to fear for my honor, for I tended to freeze flesh with my bare skin. Besides, if any man dared, Firedrake would wrap his blazing arms around me and threaten to burn the lot. He was able to do that because of special fur coats that Aunt Isolde had given us, ones that kept us from hurting the other.

When fall paled into winter, Firedrake and I would take our services to the mountains, this time to assist the church. Often villagers fell victim to avalanches and the monks would send searchers and large dogs to rescue the buried. My light feet and frosty skin allowed me to explore the coldest crannies, though I could not dig the way my dog Grigio could. Firedrake would help melt paths for the monks, so that they could reach victims on foot and transfer them to stretchers.

That day when my life changed, mountain cold had painted the sky a cruel blue. Winds froze the knots on men's jackets and sprouted icicles on their fur coats. Brother Glenn, the head rescuer and my overseer, had to thaw his dog's nostrils by covering them with his hands. He wore leather gloves and sheepskin boots that day, and a red kerchief covered his nose and mouth. His companions, Brothers Alden and Boroughs, tightened the knots on the sleigh so that we kept the injured tied to their stretchers and unable to fall off.

"It's not natural," Alden muttered. "These gusts, they say that demons ride on them."

"I'd pity the demon that did so," Firedrake remarked with an obstinate grin. "Come now, such winds would knock him helter-skelter."

"How can we profess to know how angels or demons fly?" Alden asked. "That is blasphemous."

"So is proclaiming that demons ride on the winds."

I was the only comfortable person, for even Firedrake did not like the cold trudges. My feet allowed me to skip over the snow and keep pace with the horses. In addition to the light fur that allowed me to hug Firedrake, I wore a light orange gown that allowed men to find me in the cold. I sang to keep their spirits up and often went ahead to scout the snow-buried trail.

"Hey, Sister Snowdrop, why don't you dance a path for us?" Boroughs called. "Since you seem so at ease without the sleigh."

"I'll go ahead, Brother," I replied, hiding my smile. Boroughs often confessed jealousy of my high spirits to the priest, but he knew that if I meant harm that I would've let buried men freeze in the avalanches. Besides, the Devil's women, witches who signed the blasphemous black book in blood, could not pray to a loving God, or so the monks said. My aunt Isolde was one of those women.

Snow had carved a deep ditch into this mountain, with pits for the unsuspecting traveler. Grigio and Firedrake had to walk carefully, Firedrake wearing snowshoes. As a pup Grigio had enjoyed bouncing through the snow, but he sniffed the ground and waited for my signals. Nevertheless, he kept my pace. His sniffs filled the air.

Many months have passed since then, but I'm still not sure what changed. One moment, I was skipping ahead, sensing that a body was nearby. The next, a white fog cut between the boys and me so that it breathed icicles down my dress. I whirled around. Grigio barked. It was a thick fog, the kind that simmers on bustling harbors and smothers the faintest bit of warm air. The fog muffled my brother's cries as he called for me, but not the sleigh bells that I suddenly heard. Grigio growled at the new sound.

Another sleigh cut behind us; it was larger and more ornate than the simple one for the monks. It had bone-white dogs as large as horses, and bells shaped like frozen trees. Its rider was a large man with blue spheres for eyes, an ice-flecked beard, and a large mouth. He was large and fat, and handsome for his weight.

"Good day, fair maiden. Are you cold?"

"Good day, sir, and no," I said. "We are searching for avalanche victims. Do you search as well, for kin or companions?"

He gave a wide grin in response. Grigio barked at the strange man and started to dig; he had found someone. I knelt by him and blew on the whistle around my neck.

"Fair maiden, are you cold?"

"No," I answered curtly, as Grigio unearthed a groaning head. We worked to get the body out, and to see if others were underneath.

"Fair maiden, are you cold?"

"No, but this gentleman certainly is," I responded, trying to keep my temper. "It seems I've lost my companions. Is your sleigh large enough for this injured man?"

The sleigh rider considered, scratching ice out of his beard. I saw snowflakes flutter at the edge of his snow runners, and dance to the ends of the banks.

"I have never seen a girl like you before," he said simply. "I must see you again, maiden."

With that, he yanked at the reins, and his dogs took off. Grigio bared his teeth at them as the fog flew away and towards the strange sleigh. Soon the sound of bells faded.

"Snowdrop!" Firedrake called. "You found one!"

"Yes, I found one," I said irritably, my decorum forgotten. "Now are you going to help me or play in the snow?"

Firedrake hurried with a stretcher, to help me ease the poor man out of the treacherous snow. He was red-faced and muttering something as we poured hot ale down his throat and caused him to splutter.

"Poor chap," Firedrake muttered. "Lucky for the blighter that the fog didn't block you from getting to him."

"And lucky that the fog didn't stay," I said, tying the man down and wrapping him in blankets.

Brother Alden was checking the runner marks that the strange sleigh rider had left. Relieved of duty, Grigio sneezed at the tracks and showed Alden where the man had appeared. The monk looked suspicious at the runner tracks, and crossed himself. So did Firedrake.

"I believe we've met a demon," Alden said. "An extremely powerful one."

"If he were a demon, he didn't do much," I replied. "Spoke nonsense, is what he spoke."

Yet that voice asked if I were cold. He had been obsessed with that. These thoughts I kept to myself, however, for reasons I could not have explained. Firedrake saw my perturbed face, and his eyes darkened. The edges of his clothes made the cold air around us steam.

"You have that look about you, like you know when an icicle's about to impale a poor sod," he said. "I hope whoever that demon was, that he never shows up again. These paths are cold enough without sorts like him haunting the roads."

"With luck, we'll never see him again," Alden said. "But we should save our luck for this poor gentleman, for he is breathing and shivering."

We moved to get our rescued gentleman to safety, now that we had poured brandy down his throat and helped him recover his senses. A cold wind followed us, however, like one of the straying puppies before they were trained to join us on rescues. The small gust avoided Firedrake, who blazed like a sauna once he took off his furs, and Alden grasped at his cross necklace, so I allowed the wind to wrap around me. I could not feel its chill, only hear its howling plea.

What is your name, fair maiden?

I answered in a low whisper, and the wind dissipated. Firedrake frowned at me but said nothing.

*

Several months later, a late spring emerged. Firedrake and I returned to our log cabin, our work for the winter done. Firedrake started baking loaves again, and I took up sewing and assisting my mother with the household chores. The snow took a long time to melt, and I spent as much time as I could outside with the last remaining flakes. I left no footprints on these dwindling banks, and I thought that no one could see me.

I thought wrong, and I realize that now. During my haunts, I swore that the snow reacted as I stepped on it, swelling and sinking as I walked. It was as though there were a great beast, living under the snow, breathing slowly; so I tried to tread more softly. At times strange shadows would appear, silhouettes of strange men and the ringing of snowbells. I'd call to these men, ask if they needed shelter. Fear never took hold of my insides, for I feared no man.

Then the flowers appeared. Little white flowers with drooping heads, blossoming in small circles. They had little petals, and only grew in the snowbanks.

On one day, fields of them sprouted beneath my feet. As I walked, they would bloom, and their leaves would caress me. They seemed to know who I was and wanted to feel my skin. It was as if they were carved from gentle ice, for they were cold but not cruel.

"Snowdrop . . ." I whispered. *A delicate, pure flower which was my namesake.* I whispered to the wind which carried my name back into the snowcapped mountains.

I knelt down and stroked a flower. It shuddered at my touch and perked up. I couldn't help but inhale the rich scent of fresh spring, combined with the smell of chilling ice. In the distance, a man chuckled with a deep, rich laugh. An ordinary woman would've shivered, but I listened and smiled.

Firedrake noticed the flowers, because they creeped up to our doorstep. Their petals fluttered with innocence. He made faces at them, more so because he knew that they were growing out of season. They did not like how his bare skin scorched their green stems so that they charred. He started plucking them on purpose to inspect them.

"This is a funny business," he muttered. "Since when do flowers grow all around you, and not during their time?"

"Since when does flour cling to you?" I retorted, brushing bakery dust off his shoulders. "When was the last time you got all those crumbs off you?"

"I only bathe once a week," he said. "That's all a good man needs to stay clean. But that's not answering my question."

"I don't know what's causing the snowdrops to appear," I said. "You know I'm an ice queen, not a flower girl."

"Surely you must since they seem to like you."

"I really don't." I swatted him again. "You seem to enjoy doubting your own sister."

He laughed then, but it was not a happy laugh. Suspicion and doubt filled his eyes; perhaps he suspected that I was keeping secrets.

Perhaps I was, but it's not easy to tell your twin brother that men in the shadows are causing flowers to bloom beneath your feet.

*

After the flowers came candies. Long, sticky maple candies wrapped in pine tree needles and dangling from thin branches. The wind beat the pine tree branches into dropping the candies just as I walked by, so that by the time I arrived home I'd have enough maple strands to feed several villages worth of children. The orphanages soon loved seeing me visit, for I would bring candies to the toddlers and eat with them as if I had grown up among them. The matrons kept asking for the recipe.

Letters soon arrived as well, elegant ones that spoke of my "light feet" and "shimmering blond locks". The pine trees would drop these sheets of parchment on my head, sometimes several times a week. I barely knew how to respond, for no man had thought or dared to compliment me, but they kept coming. Each one warmed my heart to know that someone thought I was beautiful. Monks tended to not express such tempting thoughts.

The more complimented I felt, however, the more jealous Firedrake became. His eyes started to narrow every day, and he'd ask me when he should start carving false teeth, since the maple candies would cause my old ones to fall out. The few letters that I left strewn in the cabin ended up in the fireplace, but he would deny putting them there. He started whispering to my father about how unnatural these gifts were.

"This is all unusual," my father said; he had that hard gleam in his eyes that said he was concentrating. "Isolde, do you know what creature has been giving you tokens?"

It was serious, because Father didn't call me Isolde unless he was solemn. We were sitting around the dining table, wrapping up our evening meal. Mother was sewing new socks for Firedrake, who stared at me with blazing eyes.

"I don't," I answered honestly. "I only have an idea. He's never shown his face to me."

Father's gleam hardened as I told him about the strange sleigh-rider from the mountains. Mother's sewing slowed. Firedrake gave a

58

bitter, triumphant smile.

"I have heard of this man, from your aunt," Father said. "They say that his horses are the winter storms, and that his mere breath will freeze men into blocks of ice. He has no heart, only an empty hole in his chest, and he cares nothing for us common mortals below, Isolde. The Frost King is the one that has been courting you."

He gave me an expectant look, as if I should gasp and wring my hands in horror. I instead stared at him.

"The Frost King? There's more than one being affiliated with the winter?" I have to admit, I did sound frustrated.

Mother looked up from her sewing. Spots of red dotted her cheeks, but she turned away when Father glanced at her.

"Of course there are," she said shortly. "Everyone knows that."

"That's not the point." Father had a commanding tone. "He's not human, Isolde, and he cannot be truly interested in you."

That stung. Father seemed not to notice.

"You're going to enter the convent when you come of age, and serve our Lord, because you are accomplished in the snow, and what man would want you? You can't even bear children, and I can't afford a dowry for you. Any husband would become the laughingstock of our village."

Tears nipped at the corners of my eyes. Firedrake came over, looking uncomfortable. If he had enjoyed tattling about the gifts to Father, he did not enjoy the poisoned words entering the atmosphere. I felt his arms wrapped in fur, but they did not reassure me.

"That's enough," he said curtly. "Snowdrop knows better for now."

"Yes, I do know better," I said, looking at the table.

It was the truth. I knew that my family didn't want me to be happy. So what if the Frost King didn't have true love? Why couldn't a man with no heart call me beautiful?

*

The next day, I set out early in my fur, and walked deliberately into the woods, leaving as few footprints as I could. I wished that Grigio were with me, but the monks preferred to have his happy company and wouldn't let me bring him down from the mountains.

When I got to the deepest patch of snow that I could find, I walked around it until I saw the shadow that had followed me for weeks. I held out my hand in greeting.

"Hello?" I called. "Good morning to you, Your Highness, if you are the king."

The laughter continued, but there was a new tinge to it, mild discomfort.

"That day, when I saw your sleigh, you said you wanted to know me. You've been giving me flowers and sweets to share, and probably the sweetest words I've heard said about me. And yet I'm told that you don't have a heart, and you don't care about people."

My words silenced the laughter. I waited for a response, for a sign. The shadow beckoned towards me, and I could swear that I heard small, muttered words.

"But I like this. No one's ever . . ." my voice trailed off. "Well, given who I am, and what I can do, no man has even tried. But my father and brother think that your feelings aren't genuine, that no normal man would want me."

"They're wrong."

I jumped at the voice. It was the same that I had heard on the mountains, but for the first time I heard anger. It was like the sound of a thick branch breaking.

"You deserve any man of your choosing in the world." He stepped out, still coated in shadows. The spring months had made him thinner, which made sense to me. "I have never seen such a kind, brave maiden, Snowdrop. No woman I know can handle the cold."

"I do it because I can," I said in a haughty tone, trying to cover up my surprise. "Because I was born under strange circumstances. I think I share blood with Old Man Winter."

"That old sod," he muttered, losing his kingliness for the moment. "I ought to have known. That's why . . . you're not afraid of me. That's why you're never cold."

I walked closer to him. He had a mantle made of blue fur, and wore boots that glittered with ice chips. The flowers bloomed around us, fluttering and curling around my bare ankles.

"Do you truly care about me?" I asked. "Or is this a game to you?

Though if it is a game, you probably wouldn't tell me."

He considered this. His thinner frame made his shoulders more hunched, and he looked more nervous than I had seen him before.

"You interest me," he said. "I do not know if 'interest' means that I care. I am interested in the way that you smile at the littlest things, that you can bear the snow while many maidens faint. I am interested in that you are a snow girl, yet you walk with the strange monks that call me 'demon'."

He sounded ill-at ease. I noticed that his beard had shrunk, so that he resembled a younger man.

"You sound honest," I told him. "But I want you to come to my house."

"What?"

"Come to my house and announce your intentions to my father," I said. "He's convinced that you don't care. He may even forcibly stop me from running into you in the woods. And I want to continue seeing you."

It was out. I didn't know if I loved the Frost King, but I liked the way he looked at me. I liked the way he was trying to convey his feelings. Like him, I was interested.

*

All day, I did my chores, helping Mother with the laundry and the cooking for the week. Firedrake went to his bakery job, and though his eyes were soft he spoke with a triumphant tone. I found myself growing resentful of him and practically danced with relief when he left. Father, well, I knew the kind of man Father was so I shouldn't have been surprised. But Firedrake . . .

I thought Firedrake cared about me. I thought he wanted me to be happy.

As I hung up heavy bed sheets to catch the scarce sunlight, I wondered why I hadn't the manic, cheerful plague that seemed to infect other girls when they had suitors. Pansy, one of my few friends, had burst into tears every time a man had stopped sending her tokens. She had threatened to throw herself from the church spire, despite lacking the ability to climb a simple tree stump.

Is it because I am an ice queen? I put a hand over my chest.

Maybe I lack a normal human heart, and thus I cannot feel the extreme emotions that drive ordinary people to madness. But does that mean that I'm not human either, because of Mother dancing with Old Man Winter?

Part of me thought of telling Mother about our evening guest. I played out the conversation in my hand. We had a simple lunch of salted peas and toasted corn meal, and there was opportunity to break the news. I heard her voice becoming shrill:

"Oh dear, does he take his tea with sugar or ice chips? We're low on both since the ice farmers aren't working yet."

"You think that it's wise to invite a king to our homely abode? He may get insulted and freeze us to death."

"Are you out of your bloody mind, girl! What will your father say?"

My lips remained clamped together for fear of hearing more harsh words in the household. It was just as well, for Mother started cleaning out her things and took out the gown made of butterfly wings. She hung it with the wet linen outside, watching it shimmer in the sunlight.

"Each year I wonder if I should discard it," she murmured. "Or to take it apart and bury the wings when I think of how many creatures died, but then I think of passing this on to you. You would look beautiful wearing it."

That surprised me; Mother had never said anything of the sort before. I stroked one sleeve. The lace borders were like spider webs, but they didn't make me fear the spiders' bite.

"If we have some time today, perhaps we could move the darts and see how it fits on you," Mother said. "If you'd like."

On another day, I would've said that it sounded like a bad idea. Magical dresses tended to cause things to happen, things that would cause Father to lose his temper.

"I'd like that," I said. "A lot."

Mother gave me a questioning look and she saw the hurt in my eyes.

"I know that what your father said was hurtful yesterday, but he's not an expert on everything. Men don't know everything,

Snowdrop. They just like to think they do."

"But Firedrake-"

"Is your brother. He doesn't want to lose you, and brothers don't express love with sweet words and gentle songs. They express it by clinging to their sisters."

I couldn't have told Mother how these words comforted and pained me at the same time.

We managed to find the time to fit me into Mother's old gown. She shook the dust off the sewn butterfly wings, and told me to hold my breath as she tightened the cords. The bust was a little large, so we had to reduce it. We got to work with the needle and thread. I probably should've known that such sewing would breed disaster, but I was too upset with Firedrake and nervous about this evening to think clearly.

Firedrake came home, saw me trying on the dress with the darts adjusted and the fur coat draped over my shoulders. Covered in flour and scorched breadcrumbs from head to toe, he sneezed when he saw me out of surprise. I saw wonder in his eyes, appreciation for how the dress suited me, and suspicion.

"You look like an orange honeycomb," he said, trying to cover his surprise. "Are you going to start a beehive soon, attracting all the yellow blighters?"

"Blaise," Mother said in a warning tone. She placed a hand on my covered shoulder, so that the butterfly wings made a rustling sound. I drew away, and locked eyes with Firedrake.

"I don't like you seeing dolled up," he said. "It doesn't suit you."

That was not the reaction I had been expecting. My mouth closed and I looked at the floor, abashed.

Mother looked hurt. After all, she wasn't going to wear the dress anymore with the darts adjusted, and herself a housewife.

"Speaking of your father, when will he be home?" she asked Firedrake.

"Soon. There was a town meeting, but he should be home in time for supper."

I moved to change into my work-gown, but Mother stopped me. Perhaps it was that despite my pale skin she had seen my need to be beautiful.

"Get an apron and cover the dress. I want your Father's opinion as well and there are too many laces to undo and redo." Her eyes were serious.

I hugged her, glad that the fur coat kept me from turning her skin to ice and went to grab the apron. Firedrake disapproved, but he wouldn't go so far as to question Mother. Instead, he went to shake the bakery flour out of his hair and change into clean clothes for dinner.

Father came home and he barely noticed what I was wearing. His head was bent low and he muttered about new spring repairs for the town buildings and where to find lumber. That occupied most of our dinner conversation, so that there was no opportunity to warn him, not that I would have. Thus, when loud banging came from the front door, he nearly jumped out of his seat.

"I'll get it," I said. Firedrake got up first, however. His eyes narrowed at me, as if he suspected me of deceit, and ripped the door open. A blast of cold shot past him.

For a creature with no heart, the Frost King looked nervous as he stood outside. He was skinnier and smaller than Firedrake. His face was thinner and the crown he wore seemed too large for him, a large ornament better fit for an elegant feast than an evening visit. The blue mantle he wore covered his entire body, protecting him from the heat of spring and my brother's rage.

"Who are you? What are you doing here?" Firedrake spat, after a moment of shock.

"Blaise." Mother's voice was hard. "Don't be rude."

"This is a social call," The Frost King said, shooting a queasy look at me and noticing the dress that I wore. Firedrake saw the look, and his eyes went livid.

The room could not have fallen more silent. Mother stood up and walked with a straight back, eyes hardened with a calm anger that I had never seen her wear. Father also came up to open the door properly and let in the cold figure. He may have thought this creature not capable of caring, but he also wasn't going to behave rudely in front of guests.

"Welcome to our humble home. Would you like a drink?"

"I only wish a few moments of your time, and I will be off." The Frost King looked even more nervous as he stared at my father. "May I sit with you, away from the fire?"

Father nodded after a moment. Mother pulled up two chairs by one wall so that they could converse in relative privacy. Firedrake also pulled up his chair, however, and wouldn't go away. I would've wanted to leave, but I sensed that disaster was brewing. The Frost King had never courted a human girl, I suspected, or asked her father for permission to court her before; he may have been a scared village boy if not for the mantle or the blast of cold air.

"So," Father started, chewing his beard, "you are the Frost King."

"That is correct. And you are Snowdrop's father."

"Her proper name is Isolde," Firedrake butted in. He ignored Mother's warning hand on his shoulder.

"Regardless. As you have noticed, I have begun to court her," the Frost King said. "You fear for your daughter, for her honor and yours. You think I am not capable of love, and that she cannot marry well because of what she is."

Father now shot a look at me; I busied myself with clearing the dinner dishes. There would be a lecture later.

"I understand that a woman has to buy her marriage with a dowry," the Frost King went on, "and that seeing as your hut is plain and simple, you have no means for such a price."

I winced as I heard that. As a creature of ice, the Frost King seemed to have no tact. Father's knuckles whitened against his armchair.

"However, I am a king, and I do not require a dowry." He remained seated, hunched as Firedrake leaned in closer. "In fact, given that this is a matter of honor and contracts, I am willing to provide a courting price instead, to continue seeing her since I do not know if we are ready for marriage. Our ministers of the poles would draw up a written document that would hold up in court, to guarantee that both she and I will behave with proper decorum, until we either break off relations or proceed to an engagement. If you find reason to quarrel, then you may bring the contract to us."

Father stopped clenching his chair. He now looked puzzled. As he was about to tell the King that kings did not pay to court girls, I knocked over a wooden cup.

"Pardon me," I said.

I bent to pick up the cup, hoping that my purposeful accident gave Father time to consider the Frost King's offer. Firedrake eyed me suspiciously. He then refocused his glare on the Frost King, as if willing him to melt on the spot.

"Your daughter is like no other woman I have encountered in the mountains," the Frost King said. "Such high spirits in the coldest regions, such courage. I imagine that she gets her large heart from her father."

I picked up the cup. Maybe the King didn't think my father was disagreeable and was making an educated guess about his character. It wasn't a lie if it were an educated guess.

"I will give my written word not to dishonor her." The Frost King leaned forward, seeing that he had carved himself an entrance into my father's favor. "If you wished to summon a human lawman, the document would hold up in court and I would have to pay a price-"

"Oh come on!" Firedrake interrupted. "Do you really believe this amount of dog pie?"

This outburst made us all jump; the Frost King looked surprised as well, and if not for Firedrake marching towards our guest, I would have laughed at the King's comical expression. Instead, I tried to get between my brother and my beau.

"Firedrake-"

He shoved past me. A strange anger had overtaken his eyes. I cried out as his uncovered hands brushed my apron and left scorch marks. It didn't hurt, but Firedrake had never been so careless before. He looked like a creature of the flame as he leaned over the Frost King's armchair.

"You're expecting us to believe that you're honorable?" he asked. "That you can love my sister and treat her well? You're not even human!"

This was too much. I reached for my brother's fur, to try to pull him away. The Frost King was making an effort to not withdraw from

Firedrake's blazing hands; I sensed that those hands would melt the blue mantle and the King underneath.

"You are also a poor imitation of a human being, but at least I have not mentioned it before," the King said with restrained impatience. "An ordinary human does not need to wear fur to protect others from his fire. Nor does he burn visitors who mean no harm. If I wanted to freeze your house, I would've done so already, but I was assuming that you and your father were gentlemen."

He showed no fear, despite having Firedrake's hands inches from his face, poised to strike. It occurred to me that the King could've brought a retinue of bodyguards, but he hadn't because he hadn't realized that a visit to a human cottage would be dangerous.

This is my fault, I realized. *My brother is about to commit murder, all because I asked the Frost King to come to dinner. I have to stop this.*

Firedrake's right hand drew back and curled into a fist. He was going to strike our guest, and melt him all over the floor. There was no time to get my fur coat, to protect me from the fire; it was hanging on the wall with the regular coats, and not within grabbing distance. Instead, I untied my apron and balled it between my hands. Then I reached for my brother's wrist, pulling back. Mother cried out as a burning smell filled the air, but she quickly did the same with her apron.

"Get away from me!" Firedrake knocked us away. We couldn't hold on, but our effort allowed the Frost King to stand and to walk to the doorway in a matter of seconds. He was kingly enough so that it looked like a sensible retreat rather than a cowardly run.

"It seems to me that I'm wasting my time with one of you," he said with a pointed glance at Firedrake, who was trying to shove past Mother and me. "But sir, I hope that we can discuss this further."

This was to my father, who was paralyzed on seeing the melee that had nearly broken out in his house. Father had obviously been thinking about the courting price and what it might mean for our fortunes, because he had to think of such things. Firedrake looked even angrier on seeing my Father's contemplation.

"How can you even consider it?" he yelled, and tried to charge past me. "How can money matter more than humanity?"

This time when I grabbed him with my covered hands, the apron caught on fire and his own fist flew in the air. I did not see how it happened, but there was a crack, a burst of light in my eyes, and several screams. First Mother's, and then mine.

I swayed for a moment, clutching my cheek. It felt like my skin and bones melted into a puddle of lukewarm tea. The burnt apron fell to the ground, charred and beyond repair. Firedrake stopped, fist still poised. It was still smoking. He stared at it, and unclenched it, horrified.

"What have you done?" Father shouted, leaping to his feet.

"Snow," he said, sounding vulnerable "Snowdrop. Isolde! I'm sorry!"

"For what?" I tried to say, only the words came out garbled. Skin and blood fell on the ground, *my* skin and blood, and I realized that my cheek had dissolved.

Oh great Lord, Merciful Father, Hail Mary and -

"Isolde!" Mother sounded panicked. "Isli!"

She hadn't called me Isli since I was a baby. I opened my mouth and found my legs collapsing to the floor. My head spun, from pain and shock.

"We need a doctor!" Father said from somewhere above.

"No need," a calm voice said. "And human doctors cannot fix this."

There was the sound of a mantle sweeping. The Frost King knelt beside me. He expressed no fear or panic.

"Calm down," he said, lifting my injured face. "Keep breathing. This is just a flesh wound."

Just a flesh wound? I'm missing a part of my face and it's a flesh wound?! I wanted to scream. But his hands were reassuringly cold, and they numbed the pain. I started breathing.

He then did something to my face. I heard him take in a large breath, and cold air covered my skin. The pain started to fade, and I felt prickles. Cheekbones started to grow, followed by new, raw and cold flesh. The Frost King kissed the new skin, so that it hardened.

"I may not have a heart," he said, "and maybe I do not know how to care for another human being, but at least I am willing to learn."

The door flew opened, and he left. I felt Mother toss a coat on top of me, bundling me up as if I were a small child. I felt her loosening my dress's chords.

*

When I went to the monks, they asked about the large, fist-shaped scar that covered my left cheek. I couldn't answer, though I was happy to see Grigio again. They saw the scar, prayed for my good health, and noted my early arrival; I was not due back until the winter.

Mother had supported my decision to return to the monastery. She saw I needed to leave. A pale ghost had replaced Father, or he wouldn't have agreed. Firedrake had tried to protest. I didn't listen to him.

The head monk, after hearing an abridged version of my tale, said that I didn't have to take chastity vows yet, but could spend the months seeking sanctuary until I decided to become a nun or rejoin my family. I didn't tell him the third option, what the Frost King has offered me.

Firedrake's asked if he can visit the monastery as well when the summer heat dies down. He's been writing hundreds of letters, filled with genuine contrition. I have not given him permission to visit or even the slightest response. Forgiveness does not come to my lips.

On the days that I can't handle prayer books or the chapel, I run off to the coldest parts of the mountain with Grigio by my side. The Frost King waits by the deepest gorges, with fresh snowdrops or new letters. Grigio growls at this strange man, but he never attacks. Even my dog can't heal the gouge in my heart, however, but the King tries. He learns how to love me, and I wish to learn how to love again. He would ask what colors I liked, what tree were my favorite. I ask if he has brothers or sisters, even parents, if he had a name. We take things slowly, not wanting to destroy what we have together.

Today, he said something new, while letting me braid his hair. He lets it grow long, so that icicles collect in it. We were reclined by a steep gorge, Grigio allowing the Frost King to scratch him behind the ears.

"I want to make a room for you in my palace," he said. "If you ever want to live there."

"A room? What kind of room?"

"A room where you can live, and heal. I can see the monastery is not enough," he said. "You're always eager to see me, as I always am. But I come so infrequently these days."

I leaned against him, feeling his furry mantle bristle with . He had never so much as lifted a finger against me.

"This room is so that if you ever want to live with me, to become a noble in my palace and perhaps my consort, you will have human amenities and comfort. I want to paint it in your favorite colors, and have fresh snowdrops bursting from the windowsill each day, so that you can wake up and enjoy every moment."

He had never spoken so tenderly before. Grigio came between us to create a chaste barrier.

"I would like that," I said, laughing as Grigio licked my cold hands. "Would we be married then, with a priest? Would I be your queen?"

"If you wish for either," he said, "though I know no priest that would approach me."

"Perhaps I can talk to the monks, and persuade them," I said. "You have been honorable, but sometimes people cannot see beyond the surface."

I looked down as harsh memories knotted around me. The Frost King withdrew.

"I will try to convince them," I said. "I only wish I knew what would change if we lived together, how I would change if married and a queen of the frost."

"I don't know," he said, "but I swear that if you don't like living with me, I will not throw you away. I will give you a home, and I will make sure you are safe. "

Safe from your brother, he seemed to want to say.

"No matter your choice, you will always be my queen, to be respected and loved." He patted Grigio and made the dog sneeze. "And you will always have a place to stay. I give you my word."

The Frost King had proven good on his word in the past few

months, and he could not break a promise. He had never even tried.

I nodded, and he picked up my hand. His lips brushed against my knuckles like a leaf soaked in the purest snow, and I was able to forget Firedrake and the monks in that moment.

"When I'm ready," I said, "I shall enjoy that room very much."

From An Unnamed Rock
By Jerry L. Robinette

Wriggling into the suit like a caterpillar into its cocoon, right foot first then the hand, drop the shoulder, step in and squeeze, left elbow tight against my ribs and hand on my thigh, then the hand slides up and by twisting the arm a little the elbow slips in and the left hand is in. Now point the toe and hyperextend the knee a bit, never thought I'd be glad for those Yoga classes with what's-her-name, the redhead with the incredible ass and her hair smelling of lavender, at least I got something out of all that stretching--Marcella, that was it, now clap hands and bring the gauntlets together and the front seam interlocks and seals with a hiss so I nod at the camera and Doug Frantz (who thinks he's the King of Cool but is really just Captain Corporate) flips a switch and the helmet lowers--damn, I'm using that ear! At least it clicked into place OK, now keep my nose clear while it rotates, sealing me in with the delicate aromas of disinfectant and insulating foam over the baseline reek of my own sweat, display says I'm still alive and everything's green, never noticed how bright those indicators are, somebody should put some work into the aesthetics of the Command Module. Wonder how many of 'em would turn amber if I held my breath a while, hold it long enough and I could get some of them to red, bet that'd make ol' Dougie Boy warp out, but then I'd get my hands slapped for sure, gotta be a company reg of some kind about that.

"Looks good on this end, Ron. You're green three by six, pressures within tolerances. Confirm comms and internal status, and your chariot awaits."

Yeah, I'll give you a call if I can't hear you, ya meathead, but that's what the guidebook says to ask, right, and who knows, maybe do a little song and dance unless it violates regs about keeping this as dull and irritating as possible.

"Comm confirmed and working. Internal status is green two by three. Ready for insertion, Captain."

"Roger. Initializing transfer and preparing for separation, but if

you're not sure about doing this, Ron, now is the time to say so. I can land you remotely from here and make life easier for all of us."

"Thanks for the offer, I guess. I'd just as soon do this myself." If I were any other miner would you make that offer, or are you just being patronizing because you think I'm still crying over Kelli?

"Roger that, it's your call."

He started to say "my funeral" but realized at the last minute that would be frowned upon by the bean counters who sign our paychecks, or maybe he's sure I'll take a tumble and he'd feel like it was his fault, like he pre-ordained it for me, delusions of grandeur. Ah, I love the feel of the vibration of the servos coming up through the boots of the Excursion Suit, but no feeling of motion as I'm trundled into the Lander, feels like I'm inside a cannon shell, once more into the breech, but not much firepower in my little popgun Lander; more of a shelving unit for me and the gear, the minimum for dropping to the rock, planting the factory and--physics and Cap'n Doug willing--getting back in the CM; I'm not really a Lander Pilot or geologist, hell not even a real miner, truth be told, just a guy delivering a box to a dusty potato, some carbonaceous hunk of leftover crud from the formation of the solar system, doesn't even deserve a name, Near Earth Asteroid Something-Something-Something-Five, I'm pretty sure the last one was a five, or maybe a nine. Either way, this ain't Luna, none of Aldrin's "magnificent desolation," no craggy mountains or sprawling seas of regolith, just a couple of flat spots and a few kilotons of mine-able ice, and I might as well be delivering a pizza. OK, if this hasn't locked into place yet--there we go, that feels right.

"Fledgling this is Mother Hen. I show transfer complete and control systems linked. Please confirm."

Yeah, now that I'm safe and sound in my rickety-assed LM we get all formal, almost like you know when they're gonna start recording radio traffic for playback in the media. Statuses green here, too, let's see if the thrusters are working, for what they're worth . . .just a flick, Ronnie, light touch, lighttouch. OK on X plus and minus, now Y, two for two, now the Z, flick and flick, good, this'll make him so happy, wouldn't want to ruin his big separation speech, and still solid green across the board, nuthin' could be finer--

"Switching video to landing mode, Fledgling. Please confirm."

"Roger that Mother Hen, video confirmed, looks like we're open for business. Thrusters all test positive and all indicators green on this end."

Carbonaceous crud, leftover building blocks. . .

"Synced with target at one point six kilometers, point oh two crossrange, two minutes from separation on your mark, Fledgling."

. . . potato-shaped lump of dirt and dust, in ultra-high contrast in the video screen on the inner bulkhead, no color and almost no texture but exotic all the same, alien soil for all its lifelessness....

"Mother Hen this is Fledgling, confirming all systems go, commence separation procedure . . . mark."

That's the only techno-chatter sound-bite you'll get from me, Cap'n, no more time for that crap as my little LM rotates two degrees and breaks connections with the Command Module, then a blazing swath of pinprick stars slides left as I remain static relative to my video screen, again no sense of motion but that shudder is the CM edging away, leaving me in the potato's micro-gravity.

"Decoupling complete. You are go for the first manned landing on Near Earth Asteroid 31665 and establishment of the newest extra-terrestrial mining facility, another small stepping-stone in mankind's expansion from the cradle of Mother Earth. God speed, Fledgling!"

Barf! Get some new writers, Cap'n, now excuse me while I do this, this is about where Kelli was when she lost it, too focused on her rate of descent and lost sight of her crossrange, rolled the lander and died before it came back upright, Excursion Suits can only cushion so much. But I'm sweeter than Momma's lemonade, descent is perfect and almost straight down, so at least he cut me loose clean. Got to zoom out on the video, that's a big crater but I'll miss it easy, rest of it looks flat as a plate of piss, fine by me. Uh-oh, drifting a little, here we go, light touch, lighttouch, lightlight--sweet, OK, don't over-correct now, there we go.

"Fledgling we show you at 100 meters and green for landing."

Yeah, no shit, now shut up and let me do this, 75 meters and Jeezus, where'd my video go, what--oh, dust cloud, last burst must've hit a pile of the stuff, great, now I can barely see--50 meters, slow down, Ronnie, you got this, nice and easy--

"Quite a dust plume, Fledgling. You might want to hover for a minute to let it clear so you can visually confirm your landing site is still a go."

Helluva idea, if I had clear video, Cap'n, 30 meters, rate of descent good, a bit of drift but fixable with a quick flick of the ol' joystick, there we go. Hey, that cleared my video and it looks OK, some shiny patches now, ice would be my guess, 20 meters and as light as a feather, gentle, gentle, just a touch of thrust, one last look down, and, and, and here.

"Fledgling to Mother Hen, we are down, solid, green across the board. How's my telemetry?"

"Congratulations, Fledgling. You look great from up here; set your anchors and you are go for excursion."

Dust still settling, the whole LM vibrates as the augers screw into the crust of my little interplanetary roadside rest, hope they anchor this baby good since we have no gravity to speak of, rotation alone could almost send me spinning off and that would suck. Bite deep, my little friends, we've made it this far so let's get the job done and get back, I ain't going anywhere for a few minutes, so I guess now's a good time to see if I can remember the set-up sequence for the mining unit, the CM could walk me through it but let's just try to do it our own self, shall we, just to earn our paycheck, OK?

"Mother Hen to Fledgling, nice landing, Ron. That dust plume had me shaking a little, but you're within 15 meters of target, and that's a damned fine landing. Switching all systems to survey mode."

He sounds different, must've cut out the broadband FM so nobody can hear us but us, who wants to listen to this stuff anyway, just the wheels of industry turning, grinding away, making a few bucks for the bossman by pulling water from the rocks and ain't that a hoot.

"Thanks, couldn't have done it without ya. Survey mode confirmed."

Watch the little screen and see the camera pan as I nudge the joystick, just a little puddle of gray light as we rotate through the darkness here, the vibration has stopped and all four augers show secure, time to get out of this flying outhouse and get my boots dirty, regolithy, whatever.

"Mother Hen to Fledgling, we show you anchored and all indicators green for EVA. You might want to take a minute after you step out and have a look due east before you get too busy."

"Roger, Mother Hen."

"East" just means in the direction of my rock's rotation, since we have nothing like magnetic north. Flip the lever to release the pneumatic clamps holding my Excursion Suit to the LM, that cough as they release still reminds me of the old man there toward the end, now to climb down without breaking my neck, like playing on the jungle gym in mid-winter, all coats and gloves but just scary enough to be fun.

OK, now down and, there we go, a few footprints, but nobody to take pictures of 'em, like posterity gives a damn, nothing historic here, just us working stiffs. . . ya load 16 tons and whaddaya get, something, something, something and deeper in debt . . . now what was Mother Hen talking about, due East? Holy crap, look at that! Never pictured it that big, reflecting so much light, this whole rock swimming in pale blue Earth-glow and it's just … wow. So that's what it is, what we all are, together on that balloon, twirling through space-time.

"Thanks for the tip Mother Hen. That's a nice show you arranged."

"Can't take credit for that one, Fledgling, but glad you enjoyed it. Now get to work, you've got four hours left down there."

"Roger, Mother Hen."

*

That should hold for a few decades and I've got what, one-point-four hours left, great, plenty of time to catch my breath before climbing back in, can double-check those power couplings to the solar array while I catch my breath and wait for Mother Hen to run the diagnostics, speaking of Captain Corporate he should be coming up-- yeah, there he is, sailing over my southern horizon, some ancient deity riding his parabolic steed across the heavens, and there he goes, doesn't take long up here, yeah those connections look tight, the number three strut isn't anchored as tight as I would like, but it's within tolerances, so screw it . . . .

"Fledgling to Mother Hen, installation complete and final checks show positive. Initiate external diagnostics at will, I'll wait for your confirmation before locking in."

"Copy that, Fledgling. Initiating remote diagnostic sequence now. You may as well climb back into place, these never really find anything."

Let's not get in a hurry, Ron, remember, baby steps, I'm the only thing not really anchored down right now, hey, look, I can do a chin-up, wearing three hundred pounds of gear! Ya put your left boot in, ya put your right boot in, then ya lock those suckers down . . . .

"Mother Hen here. Diagnostics all come back fine on the mining unit, and you're still green across the board. Advise when you're ready to initiate return sequence. Well done, Ron."

"Roger Mother Hen. And thanks."

*

What the Hell? How--how, slow down, Ron, deep slow breath, get some oxygen, try to think, what, oh, yeah, shit, I hit the switch for main thrust and. . . slow down, check your displays, still have air so I'm not leaking anywhere, hands and feet are working and it doesn't-- yeowtch, that hurts like a sumbitch, gotta be a busted collarbone or dislocated shoulder or something.

"Mother Hen to Fledgling, please acknowledge. Mother Hen to Fledgling, please acknowledge."

"Fledgling here, or what's left of it."

"What's your condition, Fledgling?"

"I'm OK I think, except for a banged-up shoulder, but, what the Hell happened?"

"When you applied thrust the LM tilted and then rolled. As best I can make out from the video, one of your struts never retracted its auger. That was ten minutes ago."

"Copy that, Mother Hen. I still have air and the suit appears to have maintained its integrity"--or I'd be just another piece of debris by now— *"haven't checked LM integrity yet."*

"We've got you on video, Ron. At least one leg of the LM appears

badly damaged. Are you able to try to climb out of the damned thing? Telemetry says thruster fuel pressure is dropping and we can't tell where it's going. But go easy, it may not be stable."

"Roger all that."

Nothing wants to move, damned pneumatic clamps didn't let go, switch is--damn, gotta take it easy on that side!--there we go, now try to figure out which end is up, can't see the video screen so have to work by feel, and I can't feel shit through this suit, who suggested putting us in these freaking tin cans anyway, there we go, now if that foot will come clear of whatever is . . . OK, good, there's the control panel so the hatch must be . . . ah, screw the hatch just go out between the struts, easyonthatshoulder and step down. Ta-da. Take that, you over-priced piece of government-built garbage!

"Fledgling to Mother Hen, I'm clear of the LM."

Yikes, been a long time since I got a headache like that just from standing up, musta taken a real good knock on the melon. No sign of the leak, yeah that right front leg never did let go, still anchored to the ground, I wonder . . . maybe landed on ice, the friction from the auger going in melted it, and when it refroze it gummed up the works, that's my guess, man, that leg took some serious torque, looks like the world's worst greenstick fracture. What's that in the--oh, just Mother Hen coming up again, moving faster now, probably tightened his orbit to get visual on me.

"Mother Hen here, Ron. How are you feeling? And have you had a chance to look the situation over?"

"Affirmative on the eval, feeling OK, still a little buzzing in my ears and my left shoulder is sub-optimal right now, possible broken collarbone. I'm trying to think how I'm going to get out of here and mostly coming up with answers that don't work, so far. What's your view?"

"Options appear somewhat limited; Fledgling is grounded until the company can get a team up here with replacement parts. And the Command Module doesn't have the superstructure to land on anything, let alone take off."

"You telling me I have to walk home?"

"I'm saying we don't yet know the best way of getting you off

there. *Walking may not be totally unrealistic."*

"Really? So you're thinking . . . I'm under a fraction of one percent of Earth gravity. If I were a rock, I could throw myself into orbit and off of my little island paradise. Problem is, once I get my feet off the ground, all I'll have for control is two minutes of the compressed-air jets in this suit. Maybe less if they've been leaking or got triggered in the fall. So you'll have to catch me."

Don't just keep going around like that, say something. Unless you've got a better plan this has to work, or I'll just mark off a prime piece of real estate for the cemetery and start digging my own grave, that would ruin the property values, but who would want to build a condo next to an automated ice-mine anyway? There's one born every minute, I guess, and with Kelli already gone the kids could use the income from my real estate empire, but they wouldn't get much--

"Sorry to go quiet on you Ron, just reading the results of the latest simulation, and this should work fine. Basically, once you're off the rock, we just plot your trajectory, transition to a matching orbit, and rendezvous. Pretty much exactly as planned, except you leave the lander there."

"Sounds good. And what did the computer say are the chances of it working?"

"Probability of success is pretty high, better odds than you get on some commercial flights these days."

Either he couldn't do the calculation or he knows I won't like the answer and either way does not inspire confidence.

"Sure, sounds plausible enough. What's first on the new checklist?"

Of course there's a new checklist, because he wouldn't commit to anything like this without signoff from control and they wouldn't sign off on anything that didn't have a checklist.

"Practice hopping for a few minutes to get a feel for it, then go to your southern horizon, take a couple of giant steps and use the top of the lander for one last bounce, then you need about 10 seconds of maximum thrust straight up with your suit jets. That puts you well past escape velocity. It will take us a few minutes to crunch the numbers and set up our transition, and then we swing by and pick

you up."

"I gotta give you points for creativity, Doug. You must be one of them rocket scientists."

"Just a humble engineer, trying to earn a semi-honest buck. The only potential snags are you smacking into us on your way out--I will stand a little clear to prevent that--or you not having the air in the suit jets to do some necessary maneuvering for the rendezvous, in which case I may have to come out and get you."

"Who am I to argue with a humble engineer? I only have one question before we start."

"What's that, Ron?"

"Where do you think we should build the shopping mall?"

"Uh, Ron, you're not running short of air or anything, right? Your telemetry still looks good--"

"Forget it, Doug. Just doing a little long-range planning for the subdivision I'm going to build up here."

"Fair enough, tell me all about it when you get back, maybe I'll invest in it with you. Now, start small with the practice hops, you don't want to use your suit jets unless you have to. And wait for my 'Go' before you make the big jump. Clear?"

"Roger, wilco, Doug. Hopping away toward the south horizon now."

Baby steps, Ron, baby steps 'cause I can't afford to screw this up, this is definitely a one-shot deal, but at least the mechanics are simple enough, and that's more of a chance than she had . . . whoa! It's not the distance so much as the waiting to come down part that feels freaky, the body has to adjust to the timing, OK, better, still not great, and that landing was not as soft as I had hoped, gotta use the pain to stay awake, to keep focused. Wish I could run but that's out of the question in this damned suit. Guess I should be more respectful, it's saved my life so far, that felt better, gotta keep my legs from trying to rotate out from under me now. I bet surfing is something like this, only faster. And with more water. So, maybe surfing is nothing like this at all--PAY ATTENTION, damnit, you're gonna screw around and get yourself dead. Christ, landings are hard on a bunged up shoulder even in micro gravity, I'm going to take every freakin' painkiller in the med-kit when I get back aboard the Mother Hen, I swear to God. Hey, nice one, I may be getting the hang of this.

"It's about that time, Ron. You think you're ready?"

"Roger, Mother Hen. Pour me a scotch, no rocks--ha ha--and set out a few aspirin. I'm ready to come home."

"How sure are you that you can hit the top of the lander for your bounce point, Ron?"

"Willing to bet my life on it, Doug. Seriously, I'm as ready as I'm gonna get."

"Roger that, friend. And you're in the right position, so on my mark . . . Go!"

Smooth and easy, Ron, smooth and easy, four hops to the lander there's one, whoops, a little wobble, nothing to panic about, keep those legs under ya, there's two, still on line, range looks right. Need a little more height in three to get the angles to work out, and . . . . OK, here we go it's lined up, now I just need to stick the lander--gotta remember that line when I get back!--and YES! Now jump hard man, jump and then the suit jets, woo-hoo, they got juice! One-Mississippi, two-Mississippi, three-Mississippi, how gorgeous, a little Earth-shine, for my going away party, maybe Kel got to see that before she died . . . how many Mississippi, screw it, I'm clear, may as well save my jets for the link-up and just enjoy the view. Look at all the stars, so many stars and I'll probably never get to visit half of 'em. But at least I've made it this far. And here comes my ride.

Hands of Time
by Fredrick Obermeyer

When the stranger rode his horse onto the edge of the farm, Patrick Sandovan hid his third arm under his shirt and ran inside the cabin to fetch his mother.

"Stranger's on the property, Ma," Patrick said.

Alice Sandovan quit shucking peas and grabbed a pitchfork off the nearby wall.

"Stay here, Patrick."

"But, Ma, I can—"

"I said stay here."

"Yes, Ma."

Alice walked up to the front door while Patrick peeked outside through a hole in the cabin wall. The stranger rode across the field to the edge of the cabin and hopped off his horse. The man was tall and had bright gray eyes. His face was old and craggy with wrinkles, and he had long gray hair hanging down the back of his head.

"Good morning," the stranger said.

"Morning," Alice said, her voice curt.

"Are you Alice Sandovan?"

"What do you want?"

"And your son is Patrick Sandovan."

"I said what do you want?"

"My name is John Kallengar, and I would like to hire your son for a job. I've heard rumors of his special abilities."

Patrick wondered what job the man had in mind. Sometimes the townspeople made fun of him for the third arm in the middle of his chest, sometimes they were afraid of him, some thought he was touched by the Gods. Occasionally his mother and he had to move on, and he worried for her safety.

"He's not interested," Alice said.

"You haven't even heard my offer—" Kallengar said.

"And I don't need to. I need my son on the farm."

"This job could make him and you a lot of money. You could get off this farm and live well for a change."

"I already like the way we live."

Yet Patrick was intrigued. Truth be told, he didn't like working on the farm, especially with the long hours and hard work.

"Don't you want to hear what the job is?" Kallengar said.

"No," Alice said. "Now I'll ask you to get off my property."

"I'll pay you and your son five hundred gold sovereigns to steal King Barrett's crown."

Patrick stepped back in astonishment. To steal the king's crown and sell it was sheer madness. He looked back through the hole.

"We don't steal to earn a living," Alice said.

"But I can offer you more money," Kallengar said. "Just name your price."

"No."

"Maybe we could talk some more…"

"The answer is no. Now leave." Alice held out the pitchfork. Kallengar put his hands up and said, "All right then. I'll leave."

Kallengar got back on his horse and galloped off the farm. Once he was gone, Alice walked back over to Patrick. Briefly Patrick considered the job. With his three hands, he might be one of the few people who could actually steal the crown and get away with it. Part of him was tempted. Yet he knew better. Stealing was wrong. Ma had taught him better than that. Better to work a hard job and live honestly than to take that which wasn't yours.

"Come on, Patrick, back to work."

"Do you think that he'll be back?"

"If he does, he better bring an army. Now come along."

Patrick lowered his shirt, put his third arm out and left the cabin to resume his chores.

*

That night, Patrick slept poorly. He tossed and turned, imagining how much better they could live doing the job. But it was wrong. Pure and simple. Whatever qualms Patrick might have had with King Barrett, he was still the king and no man had the right to steal from his king.

When Patrick awoke the next morning, he groaned and looked

out the window. The sun was up. Strange. Ma never let him sleep past dawn, since there were so many chores to do.

"Ma?" Patrick said.

His heart skipped a beat when she didn't respond.

"Ma?!" Patrick frowned and considered using his past blink.

Kallengar wouldn't take her. Would he?

Patrick closed his eyes and concentrated. In a moment, the past appeared. He looked a few hours into the past. Pain shot through his temples. Pastblink and futureblink always gave him splitting headaches, but it was the only way he could use his hands effectively.

He saw his mother walk out of the cabin and down to the river. Patrick followed her.

Near the edge of their property, Kallengar swooped out of the woods with three hooded men.

"Ma!"

He reached into the past with his left hand and tried to grab her back. It was like sticking his hand into a fire. The further back he reached, the more it hurt.

As if sensing it in the past, Kallengar pulled her out of reach, jerked her onto his saddle and galloped off with his men.

Patrick blinked. A note lay on the ground near a tree.

"Nice try, but if you want her back, go to the cave at the Garenkol Ridge. And don't try to grab her again through the past or future."

Enraged, Patrick crumpled the note in his middle hand and threw it away.

*

Less than an hour later, he arrived at the ridge. His head still ached from the pastblink. Inside the cave, it was pitch dark. Even with pastblink, Patrick couldn't see without light. He crept on till he saw light. At most he could only reach and see about a week into the past or the future. And the further forward or back he went, the more crippling pain it caused him.

He found Kallengar deep inside the cave. His mother was tied up, and she looked horrible. Her face was pale and she was vomiting into a bucket.

"Hello," Kallengar said.

"I'll kill you!" Patrick said.

"Do it, and your mother dies."

"What did you do to her?"

"I gave her a poison. And before you try to reach back or forward and take it away, I poisoned her someplace dark, where you can't see it."

"How did you know—"

"Do you think that I'd confront you without checking your past beforehand? I gathered information about you over several months before I approached you."

Patrick frowned. "Why are you bothering us? We've done nothing to you."

"Because you're the only one who can steal Barrett's crown. I tried two other thieves and both failed."

"Help my mother first, and then I'll do it."

"No." He glanced at his mother. "I still have a day to administer the antidote. After that…" Kallengar shrugged. "…well, let's just say that you have a good incentive to move quickly."

Patrick shook with anger. He wanted to reach back in time and strangle Kallengar. And perhaps he could. But not while his mother's life was still at risk.

"All right, I'll do it. But I don't know how. I don't have the plans."

Kallengar reached back into the cave and tossed him several pieces of parchment.

"Luckily, I do. I've studied the castle for several months and looked for ways in. Here's my plan."

Patrick opened the parchments and listened to Kallengar's plan.

*

It was a bold plan. It might not work, though. He considered deviating from it and pastblinking the area to find his mother. But it would take more than a day to search everywhere, and she'd be dead by then. No, he had to do the job. Much as he hated it.

Once Kallengar finished outlining his plan, he gave Patrick a horse and a cloak to cover his middle arm and hand. Patrick mounted it and rode out of the cave.

*

It took Patrick two hours to reach the city of Caranis. Once there, he led his horse up to the castle. The city was quite busy this time of year, with the Festival of Ages in full swing. Several people were celebrating the harvest in the castle courtyard. No doubt Kallengar planned the theft for this day long beforehand. It was the best opportunity to take the crown.

Patrick stopped his horse at a hitching post, dismounted and tied it there. Although it was only the first day of the festival, the city was already packed. Thousands of people were celebrating, drinking mead and beer, eating rabbit on a stick, wild boar, squash and corn chowder, dancing, laughing, carousing. With all the activity, it was easy to blend in.

As he entered the courtyard, Patrick looked at the battle mounts. Guards stood on the castle walls and above the main gate. Fortunately Kallengar had forged a pass that would indicate that he was a visiting noble. He had said that he had his fair share of contacts in the royal court. He pushed his middle arm out of the cloak through the right sleeve. It came up short, but Kallengar had an excuse written on the pass.

When he arrived, the guard glared at his pass, then him.

"Forgive me, sir," Patrick said. "I was born without a left arm and a withered right one."

The guard looked his pass again. With his heart racing, Patrick pressed his other arms close to him.

The guard re-checked the pass, then gave it back to him and said, "Move on."

Patrick sighed with relief and walked into the castle.

The interior was cold gray stone. Inside, hundreds of attending nobles and clergy sat at tables and ate. Some others milled about, having conversations. Patrick slid into the background and saw King Barrett. Patrick had only seen one picture of him, and he looked much younger than the portrait. He had the crown on his head. The only time the king would take it off was when he went to bed.

Patrick settled in and waited, knowing that it was a long wait.

Patrick trembled as night fell. He hadn't had anything to eat for a while and he stayed low in the background, not wanting to arouse any suspicions.

Soon after the moon rose in the sky, the revelry died down and King Barrett retired to his bedroom. Guards followed him there. Per tradition, Barrett placed his father's headpiece in a glass case on the second floor's crown room. In the morning, he would place in on his head again.

The revelry continued even after Barrett retired, though it was more subdued.

Patrick crept out of the main throne room to the crown room. When he arrived on the second floor, he saw guards walking the perimeter. To grab anything in the past or future, Patrick had to be in the same proximity of the object. He couldn't just reach across space as well as time.

Before he stole the crown, Patrick past and futureblinked the general area, looking for any openings. Unfortunately, guards patrolled the area almost non-stop. Only one shift change occurred during the night. Patrick found about thirty seconds when the guards weren't watching the room.

Growing tense, Patrick waited for the moment to come. His head ached, but he forced the pain out of his mind.

When the right time came, Patrick saw a guard leave and go down the hall to the nearby privy. Apparently he couldn't wait till his shift was up to relieve himself.

Patrick took several deep breaths to calm himself, then darted inside the room. When he reached the case, he took his right hand out of the cloak, reached into the future a few minutes later, when the case was opened, and snatched the crown from the men. In the future, he carried it across the room, using futureblink to avoid colliding into anybody. Then he pulled it back across the future to a couple of seconds after the present. Then he let it go.

Back in the present, the crown disappeared from the case and dropped to the ground in front of Patrick with a puff of displaced air.

Just as it appeared, the guard hastily re-entered the room and saw him. He looked confusedly at the two crowns. Patrick grabbed the future crown and tucked it in his cloak.

"Thief!" the guard said.

He reached for his sword.

Patrick ran up to him, reached a few seconds back into the past with his left hand and snatched his sword from him. He tossed it across time to his present hand. The guard gasped as the sword disappeared from his sheath and appeared suddenly in Patrick's middle hand.

Stunned, the guard stared at him. Although Patrick didn't like violence, he had to move. He struck the guard in the face with the hilt, knocked him out and hopped over him. As he emerged from the hallway, four guards appeared at the far end of the hall.

"You there," one of the guards said, and pointed at him. "Halt!"

Instead, Patrick turned and ran down the corridor. He turned a corner and crashed into two more guards. Patrick staggered up. One of them grabbed his cloak and tore it free. When he saw Patrick's three arms, he gasped. Patrick kicked him aside, shoved the other one back down with his middle hand and continued running.

When he reached the staircase to the first floor, he jumped on the railing, slid down it a little ways and vaulted down to the floor. He hit the ground, rolled and continued running.

Above him, more guards shouted for reinforcements.

Gasping, Patrick turned and ran for the castle exit. Three more guards rushed up to the doorway and blocked his way. Terrified, Patrick spun around and ran back towards the stairs, looking for another escape route.

By the time he reached the stairs, though, several more guards rushed down the stairs and blocked his way. Patrick stopped and jumped back. More guards came from his left and right.

All of the guards surrounded him in a circle and pointed their weapons at him. Patrick spun around, trapped on all sides.

"Surrender," the captain of the guard said.

Deep down, Patrick wanted to do so. But he couldn't. Not with his mother's life on the line.

He tossed the crown into the air, over the men's head. Two of them bolted to grab it. Seeing a brief opening, Patrick bolted towards one of the guards. He pastblinked a few seconds back and punched one of the guards in the face moments before he surrounded him. The guard flew back in time and when Patrick returned he was stunned.

He turned to the next guard, grabbed him a few seconds into the future and shoved his helmet down.

Looking confused, all the guards rushed him at once. Patrick ran to the nearest guard. He swung his long sword at Patrick's head. Patrick ducked the blow by a split second, kicked his left foot out and struck the guard in his right kneecap. He howled and dropped to the ground. Patrick stumbled up, grabbed the guard's head with his middle hand and vaulted over his back. The other guards crashed into the injured guard and tumbled into a pile.

Gasping, Patrick staggered over to the crown, snatched it up and ran to the exit. As he approached it, another guard leaped out and slashed Patrick in the side. Pain seared his flesh and he cried out. The guard wrapped his arm around Patrick's neck, strangled him and brought the blade down to his chest. Desperate, Patrick pastblinked, swung his past hand back in time and hit the guard in the testicles a few seconds earlier. He cried out and the sword blow missed.

Back in the present, the wound rippled and disappeared.

Patrick stumbled out of the castle. On his way out, even more guards emerged from the streets. Patrick groaned. Did they grow all these guards in the royal gardens? How many were there?

In the distance, the gate was starting to close.

Patrick rushed down the street, people gawking at him.

"Stop him!" a guard said. "He stole the king's crown."

Several men and women rushed at him. Seeing them come, Patrick swung his past and future hands out wildly, knocking them back before or after they grabbed him.

When he reached his horse, Patrick pulled the strap free and leaped onto his horse. He turned the animal around quickly, and it neighed. He kicked it in the side and galloped towards the exit. Above him, archers leaned down from the portcullis and loosed arrows. Patrick yanked his horse to the side and the arrows struck the ground around him.

"Go!" he said to the horse, and urged it on.

Ahead of him, the gate was almost closed. Patrick urged the horse onward and ducked his head. He sailed under the gate and missed impaling his head on the spikes by a few inches. He galloped out across the field. Arrows whizzed past his head as he rode down the valley.

As he reached the bottom, an arrow struck the horse's flank. It whinnied and lurched to the ground, throwing Patrick off. He threw his present hand out and it took most of the blow of the landing, although he scraped his palm badly in the process.

He staggered to his feet and looked back. The guards were already lifting the gates and mounting horses.

Patrick ran through the village right outside the castle until he saw a noble on a horse. He looked at his three arms and blinked with surprise.

He jerked the man off his horse, leaped onto it and turned it around. Unlike his other horse, this one bucked and neighed. Patrick kicked it in the flanks.

"Give me back my horse!" the noble said.

He tried to pull Patrick off the horse, but he kicked the man away and galloped out of the village as fast as he could. He glanced behind him and saw the other men in pursuit. If he didn't make it to the woods, they would surround him. And Patrick was so tired that he didn't think he could fend them off again.

He galloped down the long road into the woods and guided his horse around a fallen tree. Beyond it, a small river ran through the woods. Patrick guided the horse across the river, hearing the men's horses closing in from behind. The water rose up to the horse's sides, but Patrick urged it onward.

On the other side of the shore, Patrick pushed the horse faster. It stumbled down a muddy hill and he nearly fell off. He heard the men crashing through the water.

Patrick saw a thick copse of trees and held the horse there. After a few moments, he held the horse still and waited, trying to hold his breath.

He heard the men cross the river and travel through the woods.

For a few seconds, he heard shouts and Patrick got ready to bolt. But then he heard confusion. Apparently the men had lost his trail beyond the river. He waited a while longer and heard the men going off into the south direction, away from him.

A few more minutes passed, then Patrick urged the horse out of his hiding spot and headed north towards the ridge.

*

By the time Patrick arrived back at the Garenkol Ridge, the moon was already halfway across the night sky. Neither Kallengar nor his men were outside waiting for him.

Patrick dismounted, walked over to one of the rocks and dropped the crown on the ground. He picked it up with his future hand and pushed it a week ahead into time. Sending it so far ahead caused him immense pain, but he wasn't going to walk into the place with it and get ambushed.

When he finished, he pulled his hand back and lay there for a bit, recovering from the pain.

Once he was ready, he walked up the hill. As he expected, they hid in the dark sections so he couldn't futureblink them. Patrick stood outside the cave entrance and tried to see what they were doing. But he couldn't.

He entered the cave and walked a few feet inside. Near the entrance, Kallengar said, "Stop."

His voice echoed across the cave. Patrick couldn't see him, though.

"Where's my mother?" Patrick said.

"Right here. Bring me the crown and I'll give her the antidote."

"First give her the antidote, then I'll give you the crown."

"No."

Patrick bit his lip. "I'm not turning it over till she's healed. Otherwise you can forget about the crown. I'll keep putting it ahead and forward in time, so you'll never have it."

"All right then. Come closer."

Patrick walked further inside the cave. Further on, torches flickered on the walls and lit the way. He walked into a circular area of the cave. Kallengar was holding her. Her face was still pale, but she was on her feet.

"Now give me the crown."

"First the antidote."

Kallengar took out a clear vial and had her swallow it.

"All right, now the crown."

Patrick hesitated.

"What if you gave her a lethal poison? I'll come back in a day. If she's still alive, you get the crown."

Kallengar's face reddened with anger. "Damn it, I don't have time for this.

"Make the time."

"Damn it, lad, I never really poisoned her."

"What?" Patrick gawked at him.

"I gave her a potion that would make her ill for a few hours. Nothing more."

"You're lying."

"Think about it, lad. If I had really poisoned her, do you think she'd still be on her feet?"

"It could be slow acting."

"Lad, give me the crown. I must have it."

"No."

Kallengar's face tightened with rage. He reached behind his back, took out a dagger placed it against Alice's throat.

"The crown right now. Or I slit her throat. And don't try to reach back, because I'll kill her." He pressed the blade against her throat and drew blood. She cried out.

"All right!" Patrick said. "Don't kill her! I'll give you what you want. Just wait."

Patrick rushed out of the cave, reached forward in time and pulled the crown backwards to a few seconds ahead of him. It popped into space with a puff of displaced air. He grabbed it and ran back to Kallengar.

"Here's your crown. Take it and let her go."

He tossed it to Kallengar. Kallengar threw her aside, grabbed the crown and put it on his head. As he did, his body transformed from a wizened old man to a young one with long, blonde hair and a thick beard. His muscles bulged and he flexed them. His facial structure changed as well, smoothing out the wrinkles.

Patrick blinked in shock.

"Who are you?" he said.

"I am really King Barrett," Kallengar said.

"That's impossible. I saw him."

"You saw an illusion. My younger brother, Fernando, used the crown's magic to usurp my identity and take my place. Until I placed the crown back on my head, he could use its power to convince anyone that he was I." Kallengar stepped forward. Patrick hesitated, ready to fight. "Thank you for getting it back, boy."

Uncertain, Patrick stepped back.

"If you really are Barrett, then why—"

"If I had come to you as Kallengar and claimed I was Barrett, you would not have believed me, no matter what I said. The crown's power is that far-reaching."

"No."

"I was hoping to appeal to your sense of greed, but when my plan didn't work, I had to take desperate measures to assure that I could regain my identity." Kallengar held out his hand. "But I swear that I never actually poisoned her."

"And the blade?"

"Merely a stalling tactic. I swear, lad, I would not harm one of my subjects."

Patrick wasn't sure that he believed him.

"Forgive me, Patrick. I was desperate."

"And that excuses it?"

"No, it does not. But given your skill with reclaiming my crown, I was hoping that you would join my quest to reclaim my throne."

"After you lied to me? And threatened my mother's life?"

"I had no choice. Otherwise, the crown's power would have fooled you." Kallengar bowed his head. "But then I can't blame you for being angry. Were I in your position, I would feel the same way. Still, I hope that you could let your feelings pass for the greater good of the kingdom."

"No," Patrick said. "Not after what you did to her."

"Patrick, he's the king!" Alice said.

"I don't care who he is. I'm not going to fight for someone who lies to me."

"That is your right." Kallengar gestured to the cave exit. "In that case, I leave you in peace."

Kallengar walked out of the cave. Part of Patrick wanted to snatch the crown away, but what would be the point. Let King Barrett fight and win his own battles. Patrick refused to be toyed with anymore, regardless of whatever patriotic speeches the king might make.

"Come on, mother, let's go home."

Patrick held out his middle hand. His mother gripped it and they walked out of the cave together.

Hard Earth
By Tony Cella

The escape pod streaked through space. An arched flame trailed the white cone-shaped emergency vessel as it barreled toward the lush green orb that hung at a gentle angle. The flames and force of the explosion hurtled through the blackness of space. The rolling flames simmered closer to the pod as it shot forward.

Inside, Lance Rickson lay flat on his back, his face inches from the neon blue hologram projected over the hatch. The computer tinkered with the pixels as it charted the pod's course. The puffy dunes of his white space suit hugged his toned muscles. The spherical helmet covered the ridges of blonde hair-each lock darkened by a hint of brown-, ocean blue eyes and a square jaw. Aside from the three jagged red lines running across his left cheek from an encounter with shrapnel during his military service, the rest of his skin was a healthy brown tone.

Ash-colored foam lined the rectangular interior of the vessel. Even though the manufacturer claimed the pods were custom fitted to the pilots, the cushions pressed close against the outer shell of his suit and the straps gripped his biceps and thighs too tightly for Rickson's liking.

Neon blue text faded in and out on the screen as the computer analyzed the spherical body and attempted to match it with the planets in its system. The word pulsed over the green planet inching closer to his vessel:

SEARCHING

With his body fastened motionless, the astronaut tilted his eyes downward to check the fuel levels. The screen glowed 73.5 percent. His gaze hung on the numbers for another second. It read 73 percent.

"That's more than enough," he thought.

He glanced upward when the computer beeped.

MATCH: 5-X0-4

OXYGEN LEVELS: ACCEPTABLE FOR HUMAN LIFE

STATUS: NO KNOWN HUMAN POPULATIONS

Before a sigh of relief passed through his lips, a series of heavy jolts replaced the ship's re-assuring vibrations. Rickson's eyes pinwheeled in their sockets before the flames engulfed the blue stars clinging to the sides of the hologram.

Chunks of metal battered the escape pod, jolting the pilot inside. Massive scraps of the main ship's rent hull dug into the emergency vessel's exterior and crammed into the twin jets propelling it forward. The craft jerked from side to side as the equal forces battled with hunks of twisted metal. Sweat flew off the astronaut's body in whichever direction the blasts battered the pod.

A pylon, one end twisted into the brutal curve of a scythe, hurtled end over end toward the pearl white pod.

The temperature rose inside the vessel. Rickson's helmet screen turned into a mottled veil as the heat inside the pod outpaced the growing mugginess inside his suit. The remnants of the main ship smacked against the bellowing jets and interrupted the propelling flow. The hologram screamed that the computer was unable to compensate for the blockage and stay on course.

The curved pylon sliced through the flame-coated vessel and gouged the outer shell. The flames from the left jet blipped out with a sudden low toned whine. The cone-shaped vessel jerked for a second then began whipping in circles toward the planet ahead.

The force of the whirling pulled the astronaut to the side. He released a strained yell until the centrifugal forces overloaded his synapses.

The pod twirled through space, Rickson's' helmet digging into the confining straps, until it cut through the planet's atmosphere. The flames kneaded the gaseous sphere as the vessel hurtled toward the terrain below.

The cone rotated sideways and spun like the holographic models projected in company ads and training programs. The tiny ship shot over the cresting ocean waves then the white-grained beaches. The pod rotated and barreled forward as the bleached sand turned into yellow stalks then hills of green.

The vessel collided with a low hump of earth then skipped across a green plateau. Each impact jostled the unconscious Rickson inside his pristine white suit. The tip of the cone dipped forward and dug into the flat grassland. Waves of dirt sprayed along the sides of the craft as it screeched forward.

The hull bleated red as the heat of darting through the atmosphere combined with the friction of grinding through the soil as it skidded through the terrain. The emergency vessel lurched to a halt, the hull stained by streaks of dirt and grass.

The pod lay, simmering in the soil, at the beginning of the tree line for a forest of thick trunked brown trees.

*

The astronaut awoke crumpled inside the pod with the straps dangling about his shoulders and waist. His boots had sunk to the floor, leaving his knees to bend until they leaned against the hatch where the hologram had been projected. The blistering pain from his joints and spasming neck muscles distracted Rickson from his returning vision as he returned to consciousness. As his sight focused he noticed thin strips of light, blocked by the occasional splinter of darkness, outlining the hatch.

He realized what had happened. The computer had been trying to land the pod in the ocean, like most space ships. It had released the straps and attempted to eject the hatch before the pod sunk to the bottom of the sea floor. If the plan had been successful, the vessel would have jettisoned his unconscious body into the alien ocean.

"The wonders of technology," he thought.

The heat from explosion, re-entry and skidding across the ground had fused portions of the hatch shut. Roots and stringy globs of metal bonded the ship's exit to the hull. Rickson wiggled about the cramped space to massage the blood into his stiffened muscles.

He was glad to hear the planet was uninhabited at first. During training he had heard stories of marooned spacemen being sacrificed to cyborg gods worshipping cults or murdered by prisoners on unmonitored penal colonies, intent on absconding with the pod's gear and useful materials.

Now, faced with the prospected of forcing open the hatch with much less than a foot of leverage, an unenthusiastic sigh wafted through the orb of his helmet.

Rickson placed the palms of his black padded gloves near the top corners, with his elbows bent like fried chicken wings. The white creases on his suit's thighs flattened into taught sheaths as he pressed his knees into the hatch. As cracks in the ridged tendrils connecting the contorted hatch grew, the plate of metal ground forward. The astronaut found enough space to extend his legs to push his boots on the hatch. Intermittent crackling peppered the pod as sweat dribbled down Rickson's grimace.

When the final strands cracked apart, the hatch shot forward and thunked downward. The rectangular hunk sliced through the charred grass below.

No longer braced between the hatch and the padding of the vessel's inner wall, Rickson dropped down as his legs flew outward. The opening jammed into the underside of his upper thighs through the cushioning of the suit. The rest of his body continued downward with his upper body swinging backward. His head bashed the back of the pod, before the fall drilled his tailbone into the floor. The force of the landing seared through the fluid filled channel of his spine. His near deflated lungs, emptied by the strain of exertion, pushed out a weak gag as the pain rippled through his nerves.

The astronaut lay half-in and half-out of the pod as pain seethed through his body. After some time he lifted his arms, which were both stiff, from cinching grip of the straps, and quaking, from straining against the hatch.

Rickson's padded fingers groped the metallic band around his neck, searching for the helmet's release latches. Slits running along the white creases of his suit pulsed as the filters squeezed oxygen into suit. The air flowed toward his helmet and filled his panting breaths.

Rickson rotated the silver knobs on either side of the helmet until the narrow metallic wings sprung outward. The oily black palms of his gloves joined the shadowy orb surrounding his head. As he started to lift off the helmet, the astronaut noticed a tugging on the back of his scalp. Individual hairs snapped, one by one, as the gentle rise broke an unknown adhesive connecting his overgrown flattop to the helmet's rear cushion. His mind was too pre-occupied with the tenseness in his neck and the throbbing pain in his spine to process the pin sharp pain until the final jerk.

Rickson laid the helmet on his inner thighs with the opening facing up. He pants mixed with the dull breeze drifting into the craft as he examined the inside. Seeing the thin coat of dried blood, speckled with curled tubes of dusty blonde hair, spread over the protective cushion made it more difficult for him to ignore the serpentine blurs in his peripheral vision. While he stared, specks of darkness flickered in his field of vision. Rickson closed his eyes and bent his head from side to side and thought about the insides of his ex-wife's thighs until he had the focus to ignore the injuries.

Rickson's chest prodded the interior of his space suit with panting breaths. Sweat inched down his face; the salty mixture pecked at the perimeter of his eyeballs. The former collegiate athlete knew he should've recovered by now.

The astronaut poked at the mini-computer embedded in the suit's left wrist, until a thin black tube whirred out of his gloves from between the knuckles of his left hand's middle and ring fingers. He lay in the pod with his legs sticking out of the empty hatch frame while the computer analyzed the planet's atmosphere. The tiny cylinder churned air through its minuscule filters until the whirring stopped. A list of elements and percentages filled the screen. Rickson nudged the fingertips of his coal colored gloves over the digital etchings until he reached the summary at the bottom.

ABNORMAL FINDINGS

OXYGEN LEVEL: BELOW AVERAGE EARTH READING

The astronaut remembered the hologram's assessment: OXYGEN LEVELS ACCEPTABLE FOR HUMAN LIFE.

"Son of a bitch," he muttered.

He gripped the sides of the empty rectangular portal and leaned forward. The heat from the hull darted through his gloves as soon as he touched it. The astronaut leaped forward and skidded down the hull. Simmering scrapes ran through his suit as he slid downward. He winced in pain while somersaulting across the heat-scarred ground.

The space pilot ended his roll in a crouch. He glanced over his shoulder at the small pod. Whiffs of steam rose from the inch of black soil, charred by the friction born heat of the vessel, that lined the crashed pod. His tumbling body had crushed a patch of brown grass in the blob-like perimeter of dehydrated prairie foliage. His boots dug into the green shoots closer to the border of trees as he stood up.

A gust of wind, sneaking over the hills from the prairie, contrasted with the remnants of the pod's sweltering claustrophobia as it grazed through the astronaut's suit and into the forest's swirl of orange and brown.

Rickson's eyes tipped upward past the swirling clusters of leaves and plumes of flame colored treetops. An arching patchwork of yellow sediment, which formed a ring around a nearby planet, jutted out of the canopy-blurred horizon. He stared at the massive body of stark red that held the sulfur-toned fragments of planetary origins in a thin rakish belt. A small blue planet, with churning specks of green rising and falling on the distant surface, peaked around the solidified body as they hung in near alignment with the peak of a rust colored mountain resting in the distance. The astronaut imagined a large chunk of his ship's foreboding black hull twisting through the vacuum of space and melding with the collection of yellow dust.

He had been the pilot and sole crewman of a hulking spaceship before the nuclear reactor powering the ship destabilized. He was supposed to keep the ship on course while it "catalogued organic and inorganic masses while calculating their trajectories to alert the appropriate agencies of potential collision with critical bodies and orbital data collection units," as outlined in the job description.

In other words, he piloted a ship that made sure space junk didn't collide with planets, colonies or satellites.

In the program's early days, he labeled the flying rocks and abandoned machinery floating through the shapeless vacuum. Images of unknown masses popped onto his computer in his section of the closet-sized command room, which he dragged from the center of the touch screen to the categorized boxes bordering the monitor. The company tracked his work, as well as those of the other Space Matter Risk Analysts, and created an automated program that catalogued the images for them. The space program kept one astronaut stationed on the ship in case the trackers detected a hurtling piece of rock or metal that didn't fit their algorithms.

"Per insurance policy mandate," he thought.

Rickson flipped open the square panel covering the mini-computer built into the left wrist of his suit. His fingers dotted the screen with fumbling jabs until it began searching for the survival kit the pod jettisoned after emergency landings. A white streak pointed across the screen in the direction of the supplies for a thick second, leaving a fading trail across the moss green screen. The next digital flare pulsed across the screen after the computer re-calculated his spatial relationship to the kit.

The ghostly compass guided him to the forest.

*

Grainy dirt clung to his boot treads as he plodded past raised roots and piles of rotting leaves. The tangy smell of decomposition teased the rims of his nostrils before gliding into the patchwork of knotted branches above. The hazy autumn sun crept through the web of dying auburn leaves, gnarled limbs and thick wooden trunks.

The slitted skin of the trees had strips of bark covering their wide torsos. They resembled the plating lining the bulky exoskeletons Rickson had worn as a marine. The sounds of rocks and bullets clacking on the sides of the mechanized armor as he charged through dusty terrains blipped through his mind in a clipped echo. The memories blurred with his recollections of sprinting down the football fields until opponents speared him into the plastic shreds of green coating the field. As he trudged through the forest, the violent recollections guided his thoughts to the blood that had coated the back of the helmet.

His thoughts were interrupted when he trudged up to a creek sliding through the dirt clumps and thick trunks of the forest. The sound of the water's creep hadn't penetrated the dull ringing straining his audial senses. The stream's water flowed in a straight line past the humps of churned soil that had built up as the flow lazed past the root netted soil throughout the years. Fallen leaves drew curled spirals in the water while floating past branches waffling against banks unearthed by the slow grinding of the creek.

The sparse spotting of moisture on the astronaut's tongue lay between gums, raw from dehydrating pants. A vestigial layer of saliva coated his teeth, but had ceased to pool in the shallows between his gums and inner lips. His eyes bulged as instinctive urges flared through his neurons.

The former marine realized he had been panting since he left the escape pod, as his boots gripped the loose granules of brown soil while he clambered down the embankment. Rickson's cheeks, glazed by a red hue and dainty slopes of moisture, rippled with heavy breaths.

Rickson kneeled in front of the thick dribbling creek. He cupped his hands and dipped them into the stream, gathering the first drink he had had since a healthy gulp of vodka lined his throat the night before. The astronaut raised the shallow water filled depression from the stream. His reflection left a gentle dent in the tiny pool lying between the black folds of his gloves.

"At least I have water," he thought before lowering his chapped lips to his palms.

The scent of bitter almonds radiating from the stream slipped into Rickson's nostrils as he gulped the water with an animalistic desperation. As he reached into the stream to collect another mouthful, the liquid dropped into his stomach.

His insides coiled.

A convulsion threw his upper body backwards as the acidic juices of his desolate gut rocketed up his throat. His eyes turned upward until his pupils fixed on the inside of their sockets. The former marine's arms slapped the loose dirt lining the stream as his body whipped back and forth.

His legs tried to extend, but, with the weight of his torso compressing them, exaggerated his body's erratic seizing. The astronaut's aching head smacked into the pebbled specked ground as vomit erupted from his mouth. A burst of unconscious strength kicked his legs straight; the inertia twisted him to the right before he fell face down into the granular dirt lining the river.

Rickson's limbs quivered as he sprawled out next to the stream. Patches of dirt stuck to the coatings of watery vomit that stretched across his white suit. His left hand shook in the slow proceeding creek. Bubbles peppered the surface as the small tube extending from his glove threaded the water through its filtration system.

After it spat out the last flush of droplets, green letters flashed onto the computer embedded in his left wrist.

H20 WITH A HIGH CONCENTRATION OF CYANIDE

*

Rickson leaned on a wide trunked tree with his boots planted in the dirt surrounded by the twisted exposed roots. The black matted steel of the electronic pulse pistol, molded to the grain of his soot-covered gloves, pressed into his chest. The astronaut shifted his torso to the right and curled his eyes around the thick tree until the circular clearing behind him entered his peripheral vision.

In the center of the arboreal free miniature grass expanse, the sun glinted off a shredded metallic duffel bag as whispers of wind tussled the curling green strands. A silver rod, capped by an orange spherical configuration of solar panels interspersed with blinking blue lights, jutted out of the torn survival kit. Every few seconds the rod emitted a beep as it transmitted its distress signal to the nearest satellites, which, Rickson knew, floated light years away.

The astronaut rotated his head until it rested between the rough patches of bark. He closed his eyes and took a deep breath as tiny convulsions breached the rigidity of his clenched grip and stalwart legs.

The former marine had lain by the river until the cyanide induced tremors seeped from his body. He had tried to scrape the watery grime off his suit, leaving palm width streaks of brown and green with specks of red over the white ridges. After the attempt at cleaning failed, he had trudged through the woods until he found the remnants of his survival kit.

After being shot out of the pod, the parachute-guided kit had wafted over the forest. The ballooning linen had been ensnared by the tangled branches of the forests' orange flared canopy and released the duffel bag into the cradling net of a tree's ancient roots. When Rickson had found it, jagged rips covered the bag's surface, each accompanied by melted spots and acrid black burns.

The heat of the crash landing had melted the inside of the kit, leaving a misshapen blob of metal gear, plastic coatings and cremated rations. Whatever had found the pack had eaten a few of the salvageable meals and scattered the shredded patches of silver in the nest of the tree's outstretched roots.

Rickson had jerked a canister of nutrient-infused water, as well as a few metal cylinders of spongy-processed meat, from the coagulated waste. He chugged the vitamin water, whose corporate logo had been singed off by the heat, down the cracked linings of his throat. The astronaut had pounded the tins of meat onto the trees' sturdier roots then pried open the punctures with the barrel of his pistol, the only piece of salvageable equipment aside from the homing beacon. The savory flavor of the goopy protein had stuck to his tongue and coated the inner sides of his teeth. Despite aches contracting his stomach, Rickson had set the last canister of plasmatic meat in the rent bag next to the beacon.

Now he leaned against the hulking mass of bark and waited for some local wildlife to take the bait. With his eyes closed, the pulsing convulsions in his forearms and lower legs faded from his consciousness. Not seeing the shakes, however, drew his focus to the pain creeping from his neck and low back. The dulled sensation in his fingers felt like a second set of gloves. The burning pain rushed from his tailbone to his feet.

The astronaut's eyelids clamped shut until a phlegm spitting growl vibrated to his ears. Rickson rested his right index finger on the trigger as he opened his eyes.

A body's length away stood a wolf-like creature with spiked blue hair that flared around two pairs of curved horns jutting from the sides of its head. The animal had planted its six paws in the ground, claws gripping the soil, as it leaned its forebody to the ground in a menacing stance. An acrid black juice dripped from the animal's pointed fangs as it snarled.

Rickson raised his pistol at the low crouching animal and tugged the trigger.

The voice of a pleasant middle-aged woman responded from a speaker on the side of the pistol.

"Charging sequence initiated."

The former marine locked eyes with the six-legged predator. The creature glared back and snapped its teeth.

"Oh..."

Before he had the chance to utter a profanity, the animal lunged toward the half panting astronaut.

Rickson rolled around the tree and sprinted into the clearing. The creature charged forward, kicking up dirt and grass with each galloping paw. Halfway from the beacon, the former marine felt the predator's teeth dig into his right ankle. A jarring pain followed the jagged fangs as they ripped through his flesh and muscle.

The predator jerked his ankle upward, flipping the astronaut forward. His forehead smacked the ground before the rest of his body hit the grass.

The former marine rolled onto his back as the blue horned wolf released his ankle and mounted him. He crossed his arms over his face as the animal rushed up his body. The middle pair of paws thrashed his suit as the predator snapped and bit at his face. He blocked a gnashing strike and jammed his elbow into the animal's throat.

The creature grunted and coughed a mouthful of the black liquid onto Rickson. A pungent acidity invaded his nostrils as the spit ate at his suit left burning dribbles across his face and neck. A blotch of odorous acid streaked across the right side of his face, etching a mirror image of the shrapnel scars on his left cheek.

Rickson yelled as a smoky mixture of flesh, blood and smoldering gas rose from his upper body.

He pulled his right hand, still holding the pistol, across his left shoulder then whipped the barrel into the creature's nose with a backhanded strike. The predator scraped at his suit as it stumbled to the side.

As its jowls shook from the blow, a cloud of droplets plunged onto the white suit's padded shoulders. Thumb sized burrows blackened the stained ridges of the suit's upper half.

His left arm wrapped around the rigid strands of curled fur of the creature's mid-section as he pressed his right elbow into its throat. The alien creature gurgled as Rickson thrust the creature onto its back.

The astronaut rolled on top of the acid drooling forest dweller. The pistol whined to signal the charge had neared completion as

Rickson pinned the creature down by pressing the barrel lengthwise across its throat. The former marine rocked the alien's skull with thunderous punches as the pistol's hum grew.

"Charge complete," chimed the woman's voice.

The astronaut yelled as he gripped the pistol with both hands, pointed the circular opening at the dazed creature and tapped the trigger. A blue sphere of force gathered at the end of the barrel before plowing forward at the creature's face.

The animal's skull exploded as the pulse burst, popping a crater into the ground. A cloud of acid burst into the air as the concentrated gravity flung Rickson backward. He skidded across the clearing, his body clapping against the uneven ground.

The astronaut's legs shook as he struggled to his feet. Pain flickered through parts of his body as he limped toward the corpse of the dead beast. Black acid trickled out of the jagged remnants of the creature's neck. The liquid burned the crater below the stub of contorted bone and veins. The same fluid had, until a few moments ago, pulsed through the creatures veins to feed its thick muscles.

"It was drooling its own blood," he thought.

The meat was inedible; Rickson's upper lip curved into a scowl.

He dragged his right ankle as he walked to the center of the clearing. The former marine glanced upward and noted a few plateaus on the rust colored mountain nearby.

The astronaut limped to the shredded survival kit and glanced down at the last tin of meat. Before reaching for the metal cylinder, he noticed a visual buzz of blue dots burrowing through the pink glob. Tiny aqua colored insects, each with four high angled legs protruding from a lumpy sphere in the center, swarmed the tin of meat. Tubes covering the center segment bulged as they sucked up the creamy protein.

Rickson fell to his knees and screamed.

*

A sparse puff of dark red dirt pulsed into the air when Rickson's walking stick struck the mountain's dusty ground. The cracked ends of the thin branch, which he had found in the woods near the clearing, dug through the astronaut's black undershirt into his armpit.

Drops of blood rolled out of the ripped-off sleeves dangling over his shoulders as the jagged edges ground into his raw underarm. The astronaut's skin now blared red from exposure to the sun, aside from where the acid had melted his flesh into bulbous grooves.

The shredded edges of the black sleeves flapped as the breeze twisted around the mountain. Even with the top half of his suit unzipped, hobbling up the rust colored summit had overheated his body. The suit's arms flapped at his sides with each stunted step. The dusty ridges of the right sleeve brushed against the bundled black scraps that covered the torn flesh and blackened veins spreading from his right ankle.

Rickson hadn't checked the spreading ink-like trails since he bandaged the wound, but it was becoming difficult to differentiate between the pain shooting from his back and the searing sensations in his ankle.

His left arm drooped at the shoulder as his fingers clenched the beacon by the thin middle portion. He had decided to climb as far up the mountain as he could, thinking the higher elevation would strengthen the signal, then wait for rescue.

Beep...beep...beep...

Listening to the rhythmic pulses of sound distracted him from the pain and focused on scanning for small rocks that would drive the jagged edges of the stick farther into his underarm.

Rickson heard a large crack when his stick smacked into the ground. The top quarter of the deep green stick snapped apart. The pressure of the astronaut's body drove into his right ankle as he crashed into the rust covered rock wall on his right. He screamed in pain and curled into a quaking semi-circle as crackling shocks pulsed through his body.

Beep...beep...beep...

He thought about how he had ended up working on a deep space junk tracker. After the football scouts had decided he wasn't good enough for the pros, he bounced around some of the foreign leagues for a couple years before enlisting with the marines. He spent years of charging through ramshackle squatter colonies, blasting flames inside hives of insectoid aliens and watching the men he had been trained to call brothers riddled with bullets.

Beep...beep...beep...

Despite the growing weakness wracking his body, Rickson rolled into a sitting position. The astronaut leaned against the dusty red wall behind him and closed his eyes.

After his last tour, he applied for the space program. He had never lost the build and mentality of a grunt and cleared the physical and personality tests without a problem. The intelligence portion hadn't gone as well. He remembered the letter they sent with his contract.

Beep...beep...beep...

His eyes hung closed as the thin shadow of the looming mountain cooled his sweat-coated body.

"Your impeccable physical condition makes you a superb candidate for astronomical exploration, but, despite your excellent record of service, your deficiencies in tactical analysis prevent us from offering you an officer position."

"In other words," he thought, "they gave you a hell of a body, kid, but no brain to go with it."

He had two choices: his current position or security officer. Rickson thought she would be happy.

Beep...beep...beep...

His breaths grew shallow as the sweat drained from his pores. The astronaut opened his eyes and watched the rays of the invisible sun cascading over the orange and red tangles of leaves and brown branches at the top of the forest. His lips quivered into an uneven smile; he thought he had caught his breath.

After he signed the contract, Rickson remembered, he told Jenny about the new job. Anger pulsed through her limbs, which had softened since her cheerleading days.

Beep...beep...beep...

She had tolerated the time away at war, the episodes at home and lugging bins full of broken beer bottles to the alley each week. He remembered the curves of disdain in her web-lined eyes, from double shifts at a local greasy spoon, when she glared at him one final time before she walked out.

"I'll get her back," he thought.

Beep...beep...beep...

A last drop of spit rolled through the cracks and peels segmenting his lips.

"Help is on the way...I'll just...wait here."

Rickson watched with half opened eyes as flocks of brown leaves tumbled across the canopy with a rolling gust of wind.

"They'll come," he thought as his chest inflated less and less of the black undershirt.

The astronaut's eyes fluttered shut.

Beep...beep...beep...beep...beep...beep...beep...beep...beep...b eep...beep...

The Job
By Justin Bohardt

1

A warm breeze coasted in from the Elysian Sea as twin suns dove down below the horizon showering the normally purple waters with a spectrum of bright colors. Four moons would soon be ascending into the sky above Lesser Erindia as well as the smaller planet's gigantic twin. I realized it would be best to be inside before the moonlight started to chase me, threatening to make me visible. Besides, a job was waiting for me in the opulent one thousand and one story tower that rose before me, the tallest in Cellicott City.

Gliding through the lobby unnoticed by synthetic-skinned robotic sentries or the decadently wealthy sharing five hundred year old bottles of wine as they ambled about the tower's Firian water gardens, I arrived at a security door. Having none of the required retinal, fingerprint or DNA inputs for the security door, I simply phased through it just as a ghost might. Once inside, I headed for the central express lifts, ignoring the gala being thrown in one of the ornate ballrooms on the ground floor as well as another half-dozen security personnel.

The lift door was closed, but the digital readout showed that it was on the ground floor, so I slid through the closed door and punched my destination into the keypad: Floor 1001. A routine maintenance check will later reveal that the lift seemingly decided on its own to go from the ground floor to the top without any passengers. It will be chalked up as computer error. So much of my presence is explained as such in these times.

It might have been the express, but the elevator still took a solid four minutes for me to reach the top floor, which was where my job waited for me. I phased through the doors into the penthouse and went to work, looking for my assignment. She was an elderly woman named Tessa Lauria, one of the richest who ever lived, and an avid collector of original Terran and Centauri artwork I noted as I glided about her home. Her library was actually stocked with books, old editions that seemed well-preserved despite it being centuries since a book had actually been manufactured.

My heightened senses heard her breathing quietly in the lofted bedroom suite and I made my way quickly up the stairs. She was sleeping in an antique four-post bed with Beta-Duranian silk drapery. The window was open and the light of four moons cascaded into the room now that the sun had fully set. Her silver hair glowed radiantly in the moonlight. A moment of hesitation crept over me and I eyed the moonlight with some recalcitrance. The time was almost nigh though- I snuck closer and sat on the edge of the bed.

Tessa awakened and turned her head to me slowly. Her eyes widened for a moment, as would anyone's if they woke up to a stranger sitting on their bed, staring at them. She should have been scared, all of them should be, but none of them ever scream. Personally, I believe that there is something wired into human DNA to recognize me for what I am, and that there is only one course of action available: acceptance.

"Who are you?" she whispered, her voice weak. Perhaps she is sick. I could have read the file, but after three thousand years on the job, why bother?

"My name is Gaius Tullius Valerius Orator," I said.

"Orator?" she asked.

"An agnomen," I responded. "A nickname from an earlier time."

"What are you?" Tessa asked next.

"A much better question," I answered with what I hoped was a reassuring smile. "I'm your reaper."

"You are Death?"

I laughed. Why does everyone assume that there is only one of us and that we are all the big boss man? "I work for him," I said. "Well, not directly, I mean my manager reports to a director who reports to an overseer and then there's... Well, I can't remember all the different levels to be honest."

"I see," she said. That seemed to make sense to her in a strange way. She probably was no stranger to the world of bureaucracy. One did not get this much money by being a school teacher. "How many of you are there?"

"As many as are needed," I responded.

A moment of fear crossed her face. "Does it hurt?" she asked.

"It's a little scary," I said. "The human mind is a strange thing. It cannot comprehend death without violence. Those who die in wars, in crimes or vicious accidents do not require the services of a reaper. As such, in order for your mind to accept that you have died, a reaper is required." I paused, trying to word this in the least frightening way possible. "We must at least simulate a violent death within your mind. But there will be no pain," I added quickly.

"Is this taking place in my mind right now?" Tessa asked.

"There is no one else around, so no," I said. "This is real."

"Why can I see you?" she demanded.

"For whatever reason, we can only be seen in the direct moonlight," I said. "Personally, I think that's what led to this myth that sunlight destroys us. It doesn't- we just vanish into it."

"I've never heard that the Reaper would be hurt by sunlight," Tessa says.

"Another confusion of mythologies," I explained as I smile and show her the fangs that have just descended from their cavities in the roof of my mouth. "It's time."

"Wait," she pled.

"Death waits for no one," I said for about the ten millionth time.

"What happens next?" Tessa asked, an urgent curiosity hidden in her warm brown eyes.

"Sorry, but that's well above my pay grade," I answered.

With tachyon speed, I crossed the distance to Tessa and sank my fangs into her neck. Her body immediately went limp, her pulse slowly vanished and her soul exited this realm for whatever lies beyond. A representative of the Ferryman's Union will pick it up on the other side of the Veil and take her to whatever comes next. My fangs retracted and I looked down at the body for a moment. There are no wound marks, of course. Only a novice reaper would withdraw from a soul and leave a sign of his presence. I can't say that it hasn't happened- we did fuel that whole vampire thing for a long time. To be fair, it was the Black Death and we were all pulling triple shifts.

Some questionable hires were made and… well, humanity became obsessed with vampires for a few centuries. I don't know if people would find the truth that much more comforting.

2

My work being done for the evening, I decided to knock off early and head over to Shallow Grave. It is kind of an atemporal pub, a little place in between planes of existence to grab some R&R without having to worry about time creeping along in the linear universes. People sadly never stop dying, so stepping out of existence for a little while is the only way for a reaper to catch a break. There are a million of these dives, all of them set up by the Organization, but I really only ever come to this one. It caters to the human reaper population for the most part. It's not that I have anything against the alien races, it's just their concept of death is…so…well… alien. The Shallow Grave is clean, bright, and I know most of the people. It's a welcome reprieve after a hard shift.

The entrances to the bar and to all of the in-between places are littered throughout the various worlds and even in space itself. They tend to be in places people don't like going, so the entrance to Shallow Grave on Erindia is in Cellicott City's underground waste repository. Miles and miles of garbage, mostly organic matter, are kept in the behemoth rooms. The decaying process apparently releases potential energy which supplements the city's fusion power supply. The stench is quite something to the uninitiated, but once I phase through a battered refrigeration unit that is curiously placed amid the organic trash, my nostrils are assuaged by the aroma of burgers and cheesesteaks on a grill.

My job has taken me all over, but I was stationed in North America during the twentieth century, and my love of that era's food has never really waned. Shallow Grave is designed in that same milieu- wooden furniture, neon lights, classic billiards and even an arcade machine or three in the back. The proprietor, a taciturn fellow named Sveg Oleson- an Organization retiree- helmed the bar, growled at the waitstaff periodically, served his own brews out of the bottle, and begrudgingly would sell a few ales on tap.

Normally, the place was a little ribald with conversations loud and raucous. However, there was a decided pall in the air as I stepped into the bar, and that was amazingly disconcerting even for one who deals in death. The bar was exceedingly quiet, but I spied a few of my friends in a corner booth with a pitcher of Oleson's best. They all looked morose.

I joined them and took note of their serious countenances before I asked, "Who died?"

"That joke never gets old," Ambrose Preston retorted. He was a preppy Princeton trust-fund kid before he got the job and still dressed like an effete snob.

"It's about who didn't die," Mohammad al-Nazir responded. The bronze-skinned reaper's almond eyes fluttered for a moment as if he were about to shed a tear.

"Or more correctly, who isn't going to die," corrected Matthew. Matthew is my best friend and the man who got me this job. He has been a reaper far longer than anyone else I have ever met and he only goes by Matthew. He wears plain brown robes and often has a contemplative look on his face that seems to imply that he knows something that the rest of us don't. Today that look is not there.

"What are you talking about?" I demanded as I helped myself to a mug and poured some of the amber brew into it.

"A job went south," Matthew said curtly.

That wasn't good. Jobs did not go south- they couldn't. I mean sure, they don't always go great. Someone might accidentally see a reaper bite into the neck of a soul whose time had come and you accidentally create an entire mythology of vampires, but reapers never failed. The entire fabric of existence was based on a simple premise: life is finite. When your time was up, you left this world for whatever lies beyond. If a reaper failed to release a soul whose time had come, it could have disastrous consequences on the very structure of the universe.

"How did a job go south?" I demanded.

Matthew sighed. "It was my fourth assignment of the day, the last soul to be freed," he began slowly. "It was a sixty-seven year old woman, terminal stages of pancreatic cancer. Her death was not unexpected."

"Hospital job?" I asked. Hospital jobs were terrible. There was something about death being so close to that place that thinned the Veil separating the reaper's existence from the real world. It wasn't as bad as standing in pure moonlight, but you could be seen by many and that could make your job harder. Reapers who were seen by too many got sent to Planecia Gravis or the moons of Eriadora, where miners or the poverty-stricken died by the hundreds every day. It was not anyone's first choice for assignment.

"Closed wing of a private hospital," Matthew said. "A few wealthy patrons, trying to cheat us for another few days." This drew a slight chuckle from the assembled crowd. All of us knew that you couldn't cheat death. "Anyway, I made my way unseen to the room where the woman lay dying. There was one man in the room wearing a white lab coat. I assumed he was just a doctor checking on his patient as he was injecting something into her IV line. I first thought that perhaps he was an angel of death, helping to ease the woman's suffering and that was why I had been summoned, but it was not that."

"Then she was just dying of her cancer then," I said.

Matthew looked at me. "The doctor left and I waited for my appointed time before I made my advance, locked my teeth into her soul and yanked it out of her body," he said.

It wasn't as eloquent as I would have described what we do, but fundamentally, it was true. "So what?" I asked.

"It didn't come out," he said darkly.

"What didn't? Her soul?" I demanded.

He nodded.

"But that's not possible," I protested. "Did you have the wrong time?"

Matthew eyed me angrily and I realized that I had insulted him.

"I meant no offense," I said quickly. "But why would the soul not leave its vessel?" I asked.

"I asked that same question," he said. "And so I followed the doctor that had injected this patient at the zero hour and I discovered something terrifying. This doctor, Lazio Capaldi, has invented an anti-agapic."

"A what...?" I asked.

"A bloody immortality serum," Ambrose Preston clarified.

"The woman I was supposed to take was Constanza Capaldi," Matthew explained. "His mother. When Dr. Capaldi injected her with the serum, it changed her fate. She was no longer going to die- may never die- and that's why I couldn't release her soul."

"You do realize what this means?" Preston asked me, a bit of a mocking edge to his voice.

I was still too astounded by the news to really hear what Preston was asking me. An immortality serum? That should not have been possible- it violated every law of nature, every faith's dogmatic law, and the definition of time itself. Every religion said the same: life was finite on this side of the Veil. The only reason time had any meaning was because living creatures were only allotted a certain amount of it. If what Matthew said was true, everything that was known about the universe was about to be turned on its head. My loftier thoughts on the nature of the universe suddenly morphed as I finally comprehended Preston's question and more important the implied statement it contained.

"Am I out of a job?" I asked.

"If Matthew is correct, then we all are," al-Nazir answered. "Whether you want to call it termination or early retirement, we all know what comes next..."

His voice trailed off and I nodded. My voice was choking with fear as I managed to whisper, "Judgment."

3

Judgment was how many of us got this job or rather how our recruiters got us to sign up for it. There is a fear common to every sentient race that none who live can truly understand. It is truly felt by everyone eventually, but only at the moment of death. The afterlife, and more specifically what comprises it, can be a fine leisurely debate among living scholars and theologians, can lead to generations of war and conflict, and can inspire some of humanity's best aspects. But at the moment of death, all the feelings of self-righteous truth or memories of self-sacrifice or dedication to faith and morality vanish and are replaced by the fear of what is to come. Will I be judged? By what rules? What were my mistakes? Will they condemn me? What if my God is not the judge? What if there is no God? What if it had no meaning? What if I did not ascribe enough meaning to my life?

So many different questions run through the minds of the dying and believe me when I tell you that none are immune. The lucky few, myself included, didn't need to have those questions answered. When Michael came for me, he offered me the choice: face the unknown and the implied judgment that entailed or take a job "freeing souls" (as Michael had described it). Given the plague of doubts that had assaulted my mind at the time of my death, I took the job gladly. Now, those same questions were racing through my brain and a familiar sensation had taken hold of me. It was a feeling over three thousand years old, but it welled within me and seized control of my mind so quickly that it seemed like it had never really been gone. It was fear.

4

Long after the others had departed Shallow Grave, I sat in the booth, nursing an ale and pondering on a memory. It was one hundred and fifty years before the conversion of Constantine, and the Christians were a tiny sect in Rome, seemingly capable only of poverty and martyrdom. I was a young man and from a household that revered Mars, the god that had allowed Roman armies to march victoriously across the known world. Devotion to and the appeasement of the gods of old had led to rich lives for my family for generations, and we found the Christian's exaltation of the weak and powerless to be antithetical to the grandeur and glory of Rome. As such, if they were so desperate to be martyrs, I was more than happy to help them in their quest.

The wolf was an animal sacred to Mars and as such myself and few other enlightened individuals took it upon ourselves to adorn ourselves in wolf skins and masks and set out to savage a small Christian gathering one night. We spent the evening crouched in the alley between two graffiti covered buildings, overindulging in wine and trading banter on the violence we were about to commit. A few bottles in, I apparently launched into a long speech railing against the evil of this new religion and the righteousness of what we were about to do. I don't remember at all what I said, but it must have been impressive. There was a reason my friends had nicknamed me Orator.

At long last, a small group of people filed out of an open doorway flanked by torches, exiting from a squat, square home made of sandstone. Most were dressed in rags and some limped their way down the street or moved with the typical shuffle of the elderly. We waited no longer. Throwing a shrieking ululation toward a gibbous moon, we burst from the alleyway, swords, knives and fists flailing.

I brought the first two down with my sword, their blood spraying across by wolf pelt. The coppery scent was new to me and exhilarating, a fuel that stoked the hatred that burned in my bones. I slashed open the throat of a third man, this one lame and desperately trying to limp away. I screamed joyously as hot blood splashed across my wolf mask and landed in my mouth. The taste of victory and of righteousness birthed a new feeling in my mind, a new desperation. One last man was attempting to escape, running through a refuse strewn street, his presence barely illuminated by the distant torchlight and a few hung lanterns. The taste and smell of blood was on my mind alone as I sprinted after him, casting my sword aside. I was a wolf, a child of Mars, a warrior animal prepared to feast on the heathen. I closed the distance between the two of us and leapt, landing atop the man's back and pinning him to the ground. With a howl of victory, I unleashed the animal inside me and ripped off my wolf mask before I sank my teeth into the weak flesh of my prey's neck.

5

Three days later, I was dead of a disease that I had contracted from the man whom I had bitten. Michael was sitting on the bed in my room, telling me that I was dying and that I had a choice to make: work for him or take my chances with judgment. Although he professed not to know anything about what lay beyond, I had the sense that he knew that my judgment would not end well for me.

"Three thousand years later," I muttered to the empty bar. "And I'm right back where I started."

Sven had apparently heard me. "You could always try for the Ferryman's Guild," he said.

I harrumphed. "I'm not union," he said. "No way they'll let me in."

"Are you sure you'll be forced to retire?" he asked.

"Apart from Michael, I'm the oldest human still doing this," he said. "And I've had plush gigs for the past few centuries. Erinidia is a bloody paradise. Younger reapers are chomping at the bit. No, I'll be put out to pasture for certain."

"Well, best of luck to you then," Sven muttered, clearly not interested in cheering up someone who was determined to be downtrodden.

I was not one to usually stay this long in the atemporal areas, but it was difficult to face going back to my job, knowing that I was not long for it. I drained the rest of my brew and my alcohol addled brain opened up to a question that had been pounding at the outskirts of my mind, desperate to find some purchase. Sober, I never would have considered violating the code of conduct. If I got caught, it would mean termination and judgment just as surely as a forced retirement. But at that moment, I was possessed of enough fear and booze to risk violating that which we reapers held most sacred.

Before my conviction faltered, I jumped up from my bench and made my way to a different door exiting Shallow Grave. This one opened into a fluorescent light lit, low-ceilinged open space, divided by four foot high walls that formed cubicles as far as the eye could see. The Office hadn't seen an upgrade in the better part of a millennium. Besides, the file-managing office drones were not fans of change and despite what management might tell you, the drones ran the Office.

A square jawed matronly woman with a chain smoker's cough

sidled out of her cubicle and walked slowly over toward me. She had thick Coke bottle glasses and wore a high necked sweater with her hair done up in a bun. "Request?" she rasped.

"File," I responded.

"Name?" she spat back.

"Capaldi. Constanza Capaldi," I answered, remembering the name that Michael had mentioned.

The drone spat. "That file's been moved to processing for deletion, once senior management reviews it," she responded.

How she had that committed to memory, I didn't know and I quickly pushed it out of my mind. Senior management had not reviewed the file yet. There was still time to carry out my plan. I muttered a word of thanks to the drone and ran to a wall with multiple doors set into it. Above each door was a different sign that said Assignments, Reaper Resources, Management (Authorized Personnel Only) or Processing.

Passing through the Processing door, I found myself in another immense room with a seemingly infinite row of shelves going out into the visible distance. In front of the long lines of shelves, there was a counter with only one drone occupying it. Her face was covered by a tribal tattoo and her hair was spiked and purple. A gold chain connected her nose ring to a series of elaborate earrings. I would have guessed early twenty-first century, but her bio-engineered eyes with their eerie pink hue weren't invented until the twenty-fourth.

"Help you?" she demands.

"I need a file. Constanza Capaldi," I said.

"It's been slated for deletion," she responded.

I stared at her unblinkingly.

"I suppose I could go get it," she said after a moment, before vanishing with a puff of smoke.

A moment later she returned with the file in hand and gave it to me to peruse. Capaldi was in a hospital on Lesser Erindia in Praetorius, just south of Cellicott City. That was lucky, I thought to myself as I handed the file back and exited the Processing division. I passed through another door that said Transport, then another that said Milky Way, and several more before arriving at a door that said

Lesser Erindia.

Walking through it, I arrived back on the planet at the same moment I had left, this time in a poorly illuminated morgue that was not currently in use. The transport system knew to send me automatically back into my region, which was not where I needed to be. It was all right though, because my next scheduled reaping was not for several hours and I had enough time to get to Praetorius, accomplish my task, and return to Cellicott City in time for my next assignment.

Moving quickly through the hospital, I exited into the warm night air. I stuck to the shadows to avoid the glow of the moons and made my way across the sleeping city to the rather quiet Tachyon Port. There were only a few other commuters in the brightly lit station and I moved among them without fear as I knew to avoid any areas with windows. Bypassing the automated ticket kiosks, I passed under a sign that said Warning: Low Artificial Gravity. A long set of marble steps led up to a platform and I bounded up them with ease, taking them twelve at a time, thanks to the low gravity.

There were only a dozen people or so waiting on the platform for the next Tachyon, which was due at any moment based on the announcements coming over the public address system. The long, worm-like airship appeared out of nowhere, clearly visible in the platform's glass ceiling, and stopped on a dime. All was silent for a few moments as the rush of sound it created was well behind it and still catching up. There was suddenly a loud roar, diminished somewhat by soundproofing in the Port, and then a voice announced, "Gravity will be set to zero in ten seconds."

Ten seconds later, the ceiling of the station had retracted and the floor of the Tachyon had opened up, an ethereal blue light emanating from it. I pushed off from the floor and floated up to the Tachyon train, grateful that the large train was between me and the moons allowing me to remain invisible. I floated up into the train, along with the other passengers, and the trap doors in the Tachyon's floor closed behind us.

A cheery voice announced, "Low gravity restored. Stand-by. Ten seconds to launch. Next stop: Praetorius."

My feet hit the floor softly just as there was a sudden feeling of acceleration and the Tachyon shot forward. The feeling only lasted a moment as inertial dampeners kicked in and immediately removed the feeling of velocity. The ride to Praetorius lasted only two minutes and soon I was drifting down through the air into the arrival station in the city's Tachyon Port. The train had departed again in a rush as I made my way through the terminus and out into the city streets.

Praetorius was not nearly as wealthy a town as Cellicott City, but the entire planet was rich (off-worlders had to pay ten thousand credits just to enter planetary gravity) and the private hospital was a state-of-the-art facility featuring the latest in cryonics, stem cell organ harvesting, and other tricks that humans used to try to keep me and my kind at bay for a few more hours. Travelling through the lobby without being seen, I phased through the elevator doors and headed up to the twenty-eighth floor. According to the Capaldi file, this was where Michael had been sent to perform the reaping on Constanza. My only hope was that Constanza's son was dutiful and still present at the hospital.

The elevator stopped and I phased through the elevator door and out into a lobby that looked like it belonged more in an office than in a hospital. The reception desk was an antique instead of the modernist plastic counters that doctor's offices tended to use. A plush rug covered the carpet and leather chairs and coffee tables adorned the waiting area. A sign in gold plated lettering said Capaldi Research Laboratories.

I was in the right place at least, I thought to myself. There was only one door leading out of the lobby and I stepped through it and started to see more of what I expected. I was in a long corridor with multiple rooms off of it, all of them full of lab equipment and diagnostic devices, and all of them empty. A few nighttime lights shed the only illumination on anything in the labs, but there was a decently bright light shining from down at the end of the hallway.

Making my way there silently, I heard an excited voice saying, "These results are amazing, mother."

There was an indistinct reply.

"You don't know what this means," the first voice said.

Another quiet mumble, but this time I could tell that it was a woman's voice.

"Alright, alright, just get some rest then, mother," the man replied as he stepped out of the brightly lit room, flipped off the light, and headed in the other direction down the hallway.

Guessing that this was Dr. Capaldi, I followed him to a corner office, remaining invisible. The office was surrounded on two sides by windows and I could see the moons of Lesser Erindia shining through as Capaldi sat at his desk and ordered his computer to activate itself and to start collating the test results. Gritting my teeth with resolve, I stepped into the office and into the moonlight.

Capaldi startled and let out a shocked gasp. "Who are you?" he demanded, recovering quickly. "If you're looking for drugs, I have none here."

"That's not what I hear, doctor," I responded. "I hear you have drugs that cheat death."

The doctor looked shocked. "How do you know about that?" he demanded.

I smiled at him and my fangs descended. I made a subtle biting motion just to make sure that the doctor had seen. Fear seized hold of Capaldi and his hand reached for an object around his neck: a gold chain with a Christian cross. I stared at the cross for a moment, and for the first time, I was hit with a plague of doubts. Grinding my teeth together, I forced myself to find a steely resolve and swallowed down the voice of doubt.

"One of my brethren was sent to your mother earlier," I replied. "It was her time as prescribed, and yet her soul still cleaved to her material life because of you."

"What are you?" the doctor demanded.

"A freer of souls," I responded.

"W-what? L-like a servant of Death?" Capaldi sputtered.

"Technically, an employee," I answered. "An employment which you have placed in jeopardy."

"And that's why you're here?" Capaldi demanded. "Not because my time has come, but because you want to keep your job?"

"You are tampering with the fundamental laws of the universe," I growl. "Nothing on this side of the Veil is meant to be eternal."

I bared my fangs at him, my eyes focusing on the cross at his neck and a three thousand year old bloodlust surged in me. I was a wolf, a child of Mars, who righteously struck down one who threatened everything about my existence once before. It was suddenly as if the last three thousand years had not happened, that every gentle passing I had performed, every kind word to the departed I had uttered, and every soul I had freed to seek its salvation had never occurred.

"And yet you discount yourself?" a voice whispered from behind me.

I whirled around and found myself face to face with Michael, his countenance looking composed yet sad. Perhaps I should have been surprised to see him there, but for some reason I was not. "What do you mean?" I demanded.

"That nothing is meant to be eternal," he responded. "We work on this side of the Veil and have for as long as humans have existed. And yet the Organization was thought to be eternal. You thought your job to be eternal."

"I don't understand," I said.

"You seek to destroy humanity's immortality in order to preserve your own," Michael explained.

I had never considered it that way before.

"Eventually, all things pass beyond and are judged," Michael continued. "It is inevitable. If you slay this man, you will only delay what must come eventually."

"You don't know what you're asking me to do," I protested.

"Yes, I do," he said. "I'm asking you to sacrifice your existence for the betterment of others."

I laughed softly. "You're asking me to take my chances on judgment," I said as I turned back to Capaldi and observed the man as he clutched the cross desperately in his hands as a single tear ran down his face. Involuntarily, I felt my canines retract back into their cavities. To Capaldi, I said, "I once spent three days dying, howling in abject agony, because of my own mistakes. A possible eternity of anguish awaits me if I walk out that door and you yet breathe."

Capaldi said nothing, but stared up at me with wide eyes.

"Your faith espouses forgiveness above all else, so I will ask you one question," I continued. "Is three thousand years enough time to atone?"

Capaldi swallowed, paused and said, "Three days were enough to atone if you truly regretted your actions."

With a sigh, I turned away from the doctor and walked back toward Michael. Once out of the room and the moonlight pouring through the windows, we vanished to the doctor, but not to one another. Wordlessly, Michael handed me a reddish-pink piece of parchment, a notice of retirement. I noted that he had one as well.

"So, we're going to judgment together," I said to him.

"I truly hope so," he replied.

Together, we made our way back to one of the waypoints between the realm of the living and our world and traveled back to the Office. As we passed through the Assignment Pool, the office drones stood up silently in their cubicles that went as far as the eyes could see and bowed their heads. We passed through the door that said Reaper Resources and arrived in a small lobby. To the right were dozen of offices, but to the left was a solitary door with the word Retirees written in cold white letters above it. Michael strode toward and I hesitated for a moment, fear freezing my mind and not allowing my legs to move. Michael turned back to me and smiled sadly as if to say everything would be all right, and then he stepped through the door. After a moment, I followed.

The Librarian
By Lawrence Buentello

The bearded man who walked into the library was not an ordinary man; not a farmer or local official seeking clarification of land rights or details of the current lunar cycle. This man, dressed in an old olive-drab uniform, walked with purpose, flanked on either side by filthy subordinates who were clearly present to reinforce his authority.

Conley had been reading at a table in the nearer stacks of books, his attention focused on the poetry printed on the mottled page, so when the three men stood before him in the guttering lamplight he was unprepared for the man's unwelcome introduction.

"I am Titus," the man said loudly as he leaned over the table toward Conley. "I've come a long way to see you, old man. I've traveled through wasted lands to learn what you can teach me from these—"

This man Titus cast his gaze from one shelf of carefully organized volumes to another, perhaps surprised to see so many still in existence in the world, or perhaps wondering why Conley housed the books inside a rocky cave. He would know nothing of humidity, or of the old man's desire to keep the library from the elements. But despite his surprise, which was disguised by a satisfied smile, he met the old man's gaze again and nodded.

"These books?" Conley said, his aged voice breaking. He seldom entertained strangers these days, only his few students, and spent his time reading one volume after another, pleased in his isolation and with the company of words. He immediately suspected this man's visit wasn't based on amity. In fact, it seemed the opposite to him, and he worried if his days of leisurely reading might be coming to an end. The intensity of the man's expression seemed resolute.

Titus studied him for a moment, and in his eyes the old

man sensed anger, though perhaps tempered by need.

"Yes," he said, "I'm here to learn from these *books*."

"What is it that you wish to learn, my son?" the old man asked, leaning back in his chair. His weathered face, framed in long white hair and beard, remained inscrutable. "These beautiful books contain much knowledge, history, poetry, philosophy—the breadth of human understanding, such that is left to us these days. What is it that you wish to learn?"

"Good, good," Titus said, and he glanced at his companions, who kept their eyes focused on the shadows beyond the table. They seemed very well trained, a trait that disturbed Conley, and confirmed his suspicions of the man's nature. "There's much you can teach me, I'm sure."

Titus straightened and turned to assess the contents of the cave.

Over the years Conley had managed to fill its dry, quiet spaces with wooden shelves hewn by his own hands, and the books which adorned them, several thousand, rescued from the devastated places of the world. This library was his charge, and the most valuable resource of the people living nearby. Most, of course, were illiterate, or barely literate, though what literacy did subsistence farmers require for survival? Indulgent reading was a luxury beyond gold and jewels, one he enjoyed, though feared might die with him. That he could trade knowledge for the little food he ate was commerce enough. His joy was found in reading the ancient poetry to the people, teaching them natural cures, describing cities and cultures from long ago which now lived only in words.

"Yes, I think I would like to learn of history," Titus said, "military history."

He stared at Conley.

"You do have books about military history, don't you?"

"Yes," Conley said evenly. "You seem well spoken, my son. Do you read?"

Titus frowned, his anger once again challenging his self-control.

"That's why I'm here, old man," he said. "I'm here for you to teach me what I need to know. If you will read to me I will learn these things. If you would teach me to read I would learn them myself."

"Learning to read takes patience, and time. Do you have these things?"

"Time is precious. I would like to learn to read these books myself, but I will settle for your reading them to me. Will you do this?"

Conley nodded, staring down at the book before him, then recapturing the man's gaze.

"You seem a man of authority, Mr. Titus," he said, gesturing toward Titus' companions. "Who are you that you need knowledge of a specific nature?"

"I'm a man of ambition, old one. I've spent the last few years gathering men under my command. I intend to rebuild the world. Don't you believe that to be a worthy goal?"

"The world has been built, destroyed and rebuilt many times. Given the devastated condition of humanity, how do you propose to rebuild it?"

Titus spread his arms and laughed, as if the answer should have been obvious.

"Through force of will, of course," he said, dropping his arms, "one village at a time. I know that the generals of old preserved their peoples by commanding them in their ways. It's the only way people may be convinced to provide the labor to achieve better things. Don't you agree?"

"Through force of will?" Conley smiled and folded his spindly arms across his chest. "I believe that is how the world came to enjoy its current unfortunate state, my son. No, force of will is not what the people need in these times. They need comfort from the trials of mere survival."

"Comfort? You say they need comfort? They need discipline!"

The cave echoed with the force of Titus' words. Conley stared at the man expressionlessly.

"Old man," Titus said after regaining control of his emotions, "weak people need the strong to lead them into better days."

"And you intend to be that man?"

"I have fifty men with me and they will do my will. They understand the nature of men's souls, they know only a strong man can change the world for the better."

"If they will do your will," Conley said quietly, "why do you need my assistance?"

"I don't need your assistance. I need the knowledge in these books. The people tell me that you're a librarian of great knowledge."

Conley unfolded his arms and indicated the lamp that cast the light within the space.

"Knowledge is a malleable commodity," he said. "For instance, I have found the knowledge hidden in these books that allows me to produce the oil for this lamp. It is knowledge that serves a useful purpose. But there is also knowledge that serves destructive purposes. I will tell you this now, my son, so you'll not misunderstand. I'll not impart knowledge to anyone that will rain further destruction on this world."

Titus smiled at his companions, patting one on the shoulder as if enjoying a good joke. Then his smile faded and he leaned against the table again.

"The people told me you'd say this," he said. "But they also told me that in these books of yours you hold great riches of information that may be used to change the world. I expected you wouldn't agree with the vision of a man like myself. But I haven't come this far to be turned away by the whims of some old fool."

Titus reached out and lifted the lamp in his hand, moving the flame nearer to the old man's face. Again, Conley's expression never changed. The flame caught the tendrils of his long, white hair and seared them until Titus moved the lamp away. He placed the lamp on the table again and laughed.

"Your fire can be used for many purposes," he said. "To light the words on the page, or to burn the words on the page. If you'll not help me learn the things I must learn of war and controlling men, then you are my enemy and must be destroyed. You *and* your books."

So this is the coercion the man would use, Conley thought. Though he had no fear of losing his own life, because death whispered nightly to him of its nearness in the air, he couldn't abide the thought of all the books being destroyed by a despot without the understanding to realize their true worth. Sometimes people were only intelligent enough to refine their worst qualities.

"You have no right to destroy these books," he said.

"And you have no right to censor the knowledge they contain," Titus said. "Your life may not be of any value to you, but I can see in your eyes you'll not let your precious books burn."

You're a weak man, Conley thought, and not of the man standing before him. He stared at the light of the lamp and hoped the man's request wouldn't be as onerous as he feared.

*

The old man now walked in his garden, the girl, Erin, and the boy, Levi, both dressed in rags, attending him. These were his students, his acolytes, though he was hesitant to think of them in these terms. Titus, too, was his student, but what each had learned was very different, and the reason they had learned it based in very different beliefs. He hoped the boy and the girl, just reaching their maturity, would remember his teaching fondly, and utilize its wisdom for constructive purposes. Titus' reason for learning was entirely selfish, justified by his militant attitude as a necessary evil for saving the world.

But the world would endure, and was in no need of salvation. Humanity's durance was only an illusion.

As they walked, Conley called out the names of the flowers, and the places in the world where they once grew and prospered. The boy and the girl listened politely, perhaps puzzled by his need to instruct them in this way, since he had always given his lessons by lamplight.

The boy paused by one of the blooms, touching the petals carefully, and said, "May I ask a question?"

Conley turned, and the girl stopped walking as well.

"Certainly, my son."

"I was wondering why you've chosen to instruct us in your garden these last few days."

"Yes," the girl said, touching the sleeve of his robe, "there is nothing to read here, nothing to learn."

Conley smiled, nodding to himself and wondering how best to say what he knew to be beyond these young ones to understand. Perhaps they would, one day. If not—

"Learning begins in nature," the old man said, "here, in the paradise of the Earth. What we learn of the universe is what we document in books. Before people kept their knowledge in words, they carved their symbols of meaning in stone, and before that, they passed their knowledge from person to person through the spoken word. This is something important for you to know."

"Why is it important?" Levi asked.

"Before the bad times, our words were kept in fantastic machines. But when the bad times came the machines were destroyed, or rendered useless because there was no more electricity. Instead of reading them for enlightenment, people burned most of the remaining paper books for fuel, because that was all they had to use. Many others were lost to neglect. One day there may be no books at all, but knowledge will have to endure. It's best to know how to find knowledge in the Earth without the written word."

"But everything you've taught us is from your books," Erin said. "I don't understand."

Conley sighed, and turned to see the beautiful flowers all around him, cultivated and cared for through the graces of all the words he'd read. He thought of his books, and all the good they could do for the people of the world; and he also thought of all the destruction they could cause. Where was the balance, if knowledge had brought humanity to this place where only fragments of civilization remained?

He turned again to the boy and girl and said, "Remember what I've told you. It may have great meaning for you one day."

"Is this because of Titus?" Levi said.

"You're perceptive," Conley said. "And, yes, it is because of Titus."

"He's a cruel man," the girl said. "The men with him are cruel, too."

"It is a very small difference," Conley said, "between the man who cultivates and the man who harvests. If they are not the same man, then the world suffers, as it has suffered in my lifetime."

"What should we do?" the boy said.

"What will he do to us?" the girl said.

He will do to you what he wishes, Conley thought, though he didn't say this. Those who could serve him, like the old man, would be his property until they proved useless; those who merely existed in his world would be subject to the whims of his power, part of the machine that maintained his rule.

Such were the lessons of history.

"Mind what I have taught you," the old man said in a soft voice. "Titus is my student, and I will make certain that he understands the responsibility of one who holds true knowledge."

Conley would say no more of Titus, so he, the boy and the girl continued their walk through the garden, the old man enjoying the naming of the things they found, and it was a good day, a very good day.

*

"Why have you moved your table?"

Conley gazed up from the book of poetry he'd been

reading. Titus stood staring down on him, his face set in a rigid expression. He'd come at the appointed time of their lesson, but the old man hadn't been sitting in his usual place.

Conley had moved the table to the rear of the cave where some of his most beloved books were shelved. Beyond Titus the bookshelves created a deep passage back toward the mouth of the cave. The darkness there was deeper, but Conley had brought two lamps to the table and had been reading without difficulty.

"I thought it appropriate for the lesson I'm to give today," he said, gliding his fingertips over the dry pages before him. "The books at this location are most important to me, and therefore most important to you."

Titus glanced from one side of the shelves to the other, then shook his head.

"What makes these books so different?"

"I love these books most."

"Why?"

The old man gestured toward the chair before the table.

"Won't you sit? This lesson may take some time to give."

Titus, frowning, finally took the seat and said, "You're not playing games with me, are you? I would advise against it."

The old man smiled. "No, this is no game. It is a very serious matter. Now, tell me, what have you been learning this past month?"

"Military history," Titus said, still watching Conley warily. "The Caesars, the Art of War, the campaigns of the world wars long ago."

"Yes, the history of war, of violence. But that history is only a small part of all history. There is also the history of religion, the history of art, of philosophy. There is so much more of history that makes humanity noble."

The old man swept his arm to indicate the shelves.

"These books contain that history," he said. "Beautiful words and beautiful images of the art that once existed. That is why they're most important to me."

"Why should they be important to me?"

"Therein lies the lesson."

"What lesson?"

"You came to me seeking knowledge of the ways to control men, and that is what we've been studying together. You're a very bright man, Titus, you learn quickly. So while you've been learning military strategy at my hand, I've also been teaching my other students what I could of the love of beauty and learning. You see, these things must balance out for me if I'm to remain faultless."

"You still haven't answered my question."

"But I have. I realize that soon you must use what you have learned from me on the very people I have taught to learn of the world in a different way. You'll place them under your subjugation, as you have placed me, and you will only use the knowledge that gives you the most power to keep them that way. Therefore, you must learn the ultimate lesson of humility."

Titus, a wide grin blossoming on his weathered face, laughed quietly, though the laugh still echoed in the cave. He leaned back in his chair and crossed his arms.

"You think you'll teach me to be a gentle leader by reciting poetry to me? You believe my spirit will suddenly be overwhelmed by the beauty of the world and I'll leave you and your people? Old man, Alexander didn't conquer the world by reciting poetry."

Conley nodded. "That's very true. Alexander had Aristotle as his teacher, a man who knew something of the poetry of the world, but all that was important to Alexander was conquest."

"And he conquered the world, as I shall conquer the world. So, please feel free to indulge in as much poetry as you like, but I know what my strengths are, and they don't include compassion. Weak men offer compassion, and the world suffers for it. I won't make that mistake, old man."

"No, I don't believe you would," Conley said, and sighed. He glanced at the lamp near his right hand, and then to the one by his left, noting the shadows they spread across his books. Then looked up into Titus' eyes.

"I expect that once you've learned all you will from my books," he said, "you'll want to make certain that no one else will have access to their contents but yourself. Such censorship is in keeping with the control of the people."

Titus said nothing.

"So I've managed to give away a few of my books," he continued, "practical books as well as esoteric ones, to those who might find some value in them. Those who might find the beauty in them, beauty that will help them endure for the rest of the days of humanity. And as for the rest of my books—" He smiled sadly as he gazed from bookshelf to bookshelf. "The rest must be sacrificed for that opportunity."

Titus, perhaps sensing the cryptic nature of the old man's oratory, stood from the chair and leaned close to him over the table.

"What are you talking about, old man?"

"It was your suggestion, after all, offered to me on the first day we met. A person can learn at any age, and from any other person, even if the other person doesn't realize he is offering instruction."

"I command you—"

"Did you know," Conley said, indicating the lamp on the table, "that the lamp has long represented wisdom? Seeing through the darkness of ignorance, as it were."

"Have you lost your mind?" Titus said, his face flush with rage. "I should strike you down—"

"Did you also know," the old man continued, oblivious to the violence in Titus' voice, "what an accelerant is? Did you know that by the use of certain chemicals distilled from nature a man may create a slow burning fuse that would ignite an odorless accelerant at his direction?"

Suddenly, the realization came to Titus' mind, and he

turned, only now noticing the glow emanating from near the mouth of the cave.

"And if that accelerant were brushed over shelf after shelf of old paper books," the old man said, "a man might create an inferno from which no one could escape?"

Titus stared at Conley, his eyes wide with fear. He stood frozen in place, at once powerless.

"Why would you do this?" Titus said. "Why would you destroy yourself and all knowledge just to kill me?"

"Because we should do whatever we can to avoid committing the mistakes of the past," he said calmly. "That is your final lesson."

"I would have made you my consul!"

"Yes, my son, I know that, too."

"You're insane!" Titus cried childishly as he turned and ran toward the rising flames. Confused by the billowing smoke, Titus vanished into the flames, and was consumed.

The old man, choking on smoke and knowing his own time was very near, lowered his head toward the book to read his favorite poem one final time in the brightening light.

Magic, Music, and Greed
by Anne E. Johnson

Licking the reeds to wet them, Beatrice could already hear a tune in her head. She placed her fingers over the holes cut in the wooden shaft, took a big breath, and closed her lips over the reeds. Beatrice blew into her shawm.

She loved the way the shawm's nasal sound made her buzz all over, as if her body were the instrument. She loved the way the sweet, snaking melodies she played cut through the silence of a foggy morning. Most of all, she loved how making up melodies to play on the shawm reminded her of her father.

Papa gave Beatrice the shawm just a few months before he died. "I bought this in far off Germania," her father said as he handed her a worn leather satchel. Holding her breath in anticipation, Beatrice pulled out a wooden wind instrument about the length of her forearm. "It's a shawm," Papa explained. "There's a legend that it was once magical. Its first owner was a boy about your age, and he could heal sickness by playing on this shawm."

"But it's not magical anymore?" Beatrice asked, disappointed.

Papa smiled. "It still makes music. That in itself is a kind of magic."

"But I don't know how to play," Beatrice complained.

Papa taught her the trick of blowing air through two slices of river reed bound with leather string. Pushing and lifting her fingers over the holes, he showed her that certain finger patterns made certain musical notes.

In no time, she figured out how to play her favorite lullaby, "The Primrose on the Hill." The simple tune sounded so clear and sad when she played it that Papa wept.

"You were born to play this shawm," he told her.

"Surely I must learn other songs," said Beatrice. "May I have a music teacher?"

Papa and Mama looked at each other and frowned. "We cannot afford a teacher," Mama said.

When tears filled Beatrice's eyes, Papa kissed her forehead. "You don't need a teacher," he whispered. "Simply play what's in your heart. Make your own special music."

Very soon thereafter, Papa fell ill. The shawm got tucked away in its worn leather satchel, forgotten, while fear and grief turned the household upside down.

And then one day, not long after the funeral, when Beatrice saw how her mother wept and wept, she pulled out the instrument and played. The simple old lullaby stilled Mama's sobbing. Encouraged, Beatrice improvised a melody. By blowing through those reeds she told about all the sadness and love she couldn't put into words. Mama cried again, but now her tears were for joy and relief.

"Your music is a blessing," she told Beatrice. "It keeps your papa alive to us."

From that moment, Beatrice played her shawm every day. In the afternoon, Beatrice led the family's goats out to pasture on the grassy rocks. While she waited for them to feed, she played. The goats skipped on the hillside, bleating as if they knew the words to every song. On the trees, sparrows hopped from bow to bow in time with the music. Even the clouds seemed to swirl like partners against the blue sky.

Beatrice played at the village market. When they heard her, quarreling couples kissed and made up. The fishmonger and the baker became so jolly, they sold their wares at a discount for as long as a tune lasted. Mothers brought their fussing, colicky babies to hear the shawm's calming music. At funerals, Beatrice played to ease heavy hearts; at weddings she played to give the new couple hope and happiness. A sweet little boy named Arval often did a goofy dance around Beatrice and her shawm, threatening to make her laugh. But she didn't mind. She was grateful whenever someone enjoyed her melodies.

One day, little Arval came scrambling over the rocks where Beatrice was minding the goats. "My baby sister!" he sobbed. "She's dying from the fever! Please, won't you come, Beatrice, and calm her and my Mama? Play your shawm for them, I beg you."

"You stay here and watch the goats," she told him. Down she ran, across the village to the hut on the lake where Arval's family lived. Even from the dirt path outside, Beatrice could hear the baby's dangerous wheezing and the mother's hopeless sobs. Approaching the open window, Beatrice began to play.

Her melody told about how sorry she was for the baby's suffering and how she wished the illness would vanish. As she played, she pictured the infant growing into a toddler and then into an energetic child who ran around the village and splashed in the lake.

Beatrice had completely lost herself in this fantasy when a shriek from the house brought her song to a halt. "My baby!" cried Arval's mother. Beatrice lowered her head to pray for the little one's departed soul. But the father came rushing outside to embrace her. "You healed our baby!" the man sobbed. "Her fever and rash are gone. She's laughing in her mama's arms!"

As the ecstatic father fell to his knees, Beatrice listened. Sure enough, mixed into the grateful weeping and exclamations of the gathered family, Beatrice heard the coo of a happy, healthy baby.

"Your shawm is magical," declared Arval's papa. "How can we thank you? May we offer you a gift?"

Too excited to worry about payment, Beatrice kissed the shawm, whooping, "It's magical again!"

She tore off in search of somebody else to heal. She thought of Old Guillermo, the blacksmith's father. She ran to the blacksmith's shop as fast as she could. "I want to play for your papa, please," Beatrice announced, panting in the acrid stench of iron and fire. Young Guillermo, the blackmith, looked up from the horseshoe he was forming and nodded.

Beatrice pounded up the wooden steps, placing her fingers on the shawm's holes to get ready. The moment she sprang into the dwelling above the shop, she started to play.

Old Guillermo hadn't walked in years. He sat in a wide chair, his swollen legs covered with a shawl. At first he just bobbed his head to the lively rhythm of the shawm's tune. But the more Beatrice played, the further her mind floated away from what she truly saw in the room before her. Instead, she pictured old Guillermo leaping out of his chair and dancing an *estampida*.

"Halleluia!" cried the old man. "My legs are healed!" When Beatrice opened her eyes, Old Guillermo was standing up, taking tentative steps toward her in his tattered nightshirt. "You and that instrument worked a miracle," he declared joyfully.

*

Word of the magical shawm spread throughout the land. Beatrice no longer had time to carry the water or go to the market or tend the goats. She was occupied constantly with healing sick or injured pilgrims who had heard about the shawm's healing powers.

Then again, Mama and Beatrice could now afford to pay Arval and his older sister to do their chores for them. The people whom Beatrice helped paid her handsomely. Not that she ever asked for payment. She just loved to play the shawm and loved having magical powers. She kept her father in her heart, and knew he would be pleased.

Beatrice and her village thrived in happiness and prosperity.

*

It's a sad fact of life that, whenever great fortune chooses a particular place to dwell, eventually that place attracts the attention of a bad element. In this case, the bad element was in the form of a troubadour.

Troubadours were poets and musicians who traveled the countryside composing songs about anything they were paid to. For the right amount of silver, they made cowardly men sound like heroes; turned shrill, buck-toothed harpies into Greek goddesses; remembered spoiled, inbred noblemen as great leaders of society.

Needless to say, rumors about a shawm that healed the sick proved a great temptation to an unscrupulous traveling musician. And one just happened to be in the region of Beatrice's village.

One fine afternoon, Beatrice was playing her shawm for a stray dog with a limp. The dog listened with its head cocked, whimpering at the end of every phrase. So lost was Beatrice in her visions of this dog romping merrily across a field, that she didn't notice the man come up behind her.

The dog noticed, however, and let loose a threatening growl. The warning made Beatrice spin just in time to see a handsome, slender man slide a lute from his back to his chest.

Beaming a sunny smile down on her, he strummed the strings of his instrument. "What a pleasure to meet a fellow musician," he oozed. The strap across his shoulder kept his lute from falling when he bowed deeply. "And you do play very well, my dear."

"Thank you, sir," said Beatrice shyly. She curtsied.

"May I inquire," asked the stranger, "as to why you are serenading a mongrel dog? Surely a girl of your musical talent might gain fame and fortune playing all over Hispania. By my oath, you could impress the most powerful of kings with your sweet tone!"

Embarrassed by the flattery, Beatrice looked down and giggled. "I have no wish for fame, sir. And I shall never leave this village. It is my home. It is my joy and destiny to play for those who are sick or injured." She held out the shawm in both palms and gazed earnestly at the troubadour. "My father gave me this instrument." Her lips trembled. "It has the magic power to heal."

"Absolutely extraordinary!" gasped the stranger. He rubbed his chin thoughtfully, never taking his eyes off the shawm. "I'll tell you a secret," he said. "I happen to think that I have some healing powers, myself. The Lord has blessed me in that way."

"Oh, how wonderful!" Beatrice gushed, admiring the stranger's strong jaw line. "Do you heal by singing, sir?"

He leaned down so his face was very near hers. "I try," he replied. His breath smelled of savory herbs. "However, I rarely succeed. Yet I'm sure that my powers could double if I were to play a magical instrument. And, as it happens, I do know a few tunes on the shawm. We troubadours must gain an acquaintance with every type of instrument, you understand."

His smile gave Beatrice a warm, trusting feeling. "Oh, please do play something on my shawm," she said. "I had not yet healed this dog's leg. Would you like to try?"

"I should be most honored, Miss." With long, nimble fingers, the troubadour reached for the shawm. Slowly he brought the reeds to his lips.

Pleased to meet a veteran musician who was also a fellow adventurer in the secrets of magic, Beatrice clasped her hands together expectantly. She was not disappointed. A sweet tone, rich as a Christmas cake, flowed from the shawm when the troubadour blew. Letting the sound swirl around her, she closed her eyes happily.

The music stopped. "Poor, stupid child," cackled the troubadour.

By the time Beatrice opened her eyes, the visitor was already loping through the village center on his long, long legs. The little dog tried to give chase, but its limp slowed it hopelessly. Beatrice slapped both hands against her chest. The pain in her heart felt like she was watching her father die all over again.

"My shawm!" she wailed. "That evil man stole my shawm!"

Every villager ran after the troubadour. Many would not have been able to run if not for that magical shawm. Even the goats and dogs of the village ran with the crowd, bleating and barking up an awful racket.

They cornered the troubadour on the banks of Lake Lanuza. "This is not fair!" he cried, holding up his hands like a supplicant. "I'll get my lute wet if I swim, and my lute is my livelihood."

"You have no livelihood now," growled Father Francisco, the village priest. "You belong in irons."

"Never!" shrieked the troubadour. He hurled his traveling bundle and stick at the priest, but Father Francisco dodged the blow. Instead of striking its target, the stick hit little Arval in the head.

The boy fell onto the pebbled shore and did not move.

"Oh, woe is me!" keened the thief. His anguish sounded genuine. He clasped his hands before his chest. "Truly, I never meant to hurt anyone. I'm just a man who loves music and poetry and a fine meal." He looked around frantically. "I did not plan to become a bad person. How did I go so far astray?"

From the waistband of his britches he pulled the magical shawm. "Let me try to heal the child I've wounded," he offered. With a sweet, calming tone he played the first notes of "The Primrose on the Hill."

"That was my father's favorite song," Beatrice sniffled. "I have never heard it play so beautifully. How can an evil man make such beautiful sounds?" She was hiding behind her mother, and peeked around her skirts. She and all the villagers watched to see whether Arval would be healed. The child did not move.

"It's because your heart is wicked," declared Father Francisco. He snatched the shawm from the frowning thief. "I may be a little rusty in my playing," the priest admitted, "but I can manage a lullaby. And I do my best to have a good heart." Putting the reeds to his lips, he played "The Primrose on the Hill." His sound wobbled. The villagers clasped their hands in prayer. But Arval still lay lifeless on the shore.

Beatrice could no longer stand it. "Let me play." Rushing forward, she took the shawm away from Father Francisco. Because she'd just heard it, she automatically began to play "The Primrose on the Hill." Quietly, the villagers hummed along. Arval showed no signs of life.

Lowering the shawm, Beatrice hung her head. "The shawm's magic is gone," she sobbed. "I can't heal him."

As the villagers moaned with grief, Beatrice closed her eyes. She pictured her friend Arval skipping over the rocks with her, chasing a goat, singing silly rhymes. In her mind, her thoughts turned into a melody. Beatrice raised the shawm and blew into it.

The more she played, the more vibrant were her memories of Arval. She could even hear the sound of his laughter.

"He's alive!" cried Arval's mama. "Oh, Beatrice! You saved him."

"I guess the shawm got its magic back after all," Beatrice explained, trembling with relief. She rushed to give Arval a big hug.

The thieving troubadour put his hand on his heart. Tears streamed down his face. "My girl," he said, kneeling before Beatrice, "you are wrong about that instrument."

She felt a flash of anger. But his tears were so genuine that Beatrice took pity and spoke to him. "Can you not see that the shawm is magic?"

He shook his head. "It is not the instrument. It's your music. It's the haunting, colorful melodies you make up. They hold life in their very notes." He smiled. For a change, it was a sincere, gentle smile. "The shawm only carries the magic that *you* make. You are the greatest musician I have ever known. Can you forgive a lowly troubadour for being so foolish and selfish?"

Beatrice looked at him and sighed. "I forgive you. Now, you must play music with me."

She took a big breath and let the beginning of "The Primrose on the Hill" flow through the shawm. The troubadour swung his lute off his back and strummed along. The intricate patterns he plucked from the strings skipped delicately around the shawm's long notes. The shawm and the lute were like two friends who had taken very different paths but still ended up together. Beatrice felt more magic in her music than she ever had before.

All the villagers sang along, holding hands and swaying. Even the fish in the Lake Lanuza seemed to dance in time under the glittering water.

Mars Ride Along
By EJ Shumak

I wake and have no idea where I am. I always wake to confusion. They said we would get used to the environment. That was as much crap as everything else about this mission.

"Мне все равно", Great. It was the Russians arguing again that woke me. Well I suppose it's better than sleeping and dreaming. This last time I woke up thinking there was still a NASA and the US led the world in the solar system.I guess my dreams are even older than I am.

I didn't want anything to do with the Russians; I don't understand why they were even on this mission. Granted we needed the Japanese, or we weren't getting anywhere. Wow, I really am arrogant, Like WE need the Japanese, Hell yeah; problem is they don't need us. Kinda neat all I have to do is change "us" to "US" and I go from personal to prewar political. If I thought us/US was arrogant, the Russians give the team nothing but arrogance and grief.

They couldn't even get along together; one of them claimed to be Ukrainian, even though there was no Ukraine. I didn't even know how or why that happened. First there was a Ukraine, then there wasn't, then there was again, then us/US got involved and all hell broke loose.

They taught us that no one believed Putin was crazy enough to loose his nukes -- destroyed nearly a quarter of Earth, The orders to launch are obeyed and then, just two weeks later, Putin is slaughtered by his own cabinet. I definitely don't understand Russians. The Ukrainians no longer had a country and us/US was just a shade better than third world.

Now I'm headin' for Mars with Russians under Nihon command and we speak American English. Three more months, and personally I don't believe there is a station there anymore. I got no use for Japanese command either. I still believe in American superiority, only a memory now.

"Duerr, I need the Davidavich relieved."

"Right, Lieutenant Commander." I get two points for that one. I didn't call him Captain, but referred to his rank, Sato hated that but couldn't bring himself to complain because I was still accurate as to rank if not command status. I also didn't mention his "the Davidavich" slip. But Daichi knew he messed up. He always knew. I couldn't wait to tell Yasue. She'd make him feel even more worthless than I could. I smiled.

Kicking off my bunk rail, I sailed through the comm station up to navigation. I slammed into Davidavich, using the back of his crash couch for a brake.

"пошел на хуй"

"Hey be nice comrade, I'm here to relieve you, not just wake you up. Watch the language too pal, we don't have a problem now, but I'm open if you are." He just glared at me, unbuckled and pushed off back down the core. Again, I smiled. It seemed to be my only defense, my only pleasure and my only option.

My buddy Davidavich left shift after doing absolutely nothing. No tracings, no positioning, hell we could be headed for Venus instead of Mars for all that lazy shit knew. I scrunched down into the cushions, trying to give myself an illusion of gravity or at least G-force by jerkin' the crash straps tight.

We had so little to do on this mission, I'm amazed anybody could avoid work. I was happy as a clam in dogshit to have something to take my mind off home. Not to mention why I volunteered for a multi-year mission that I believed was at best a waste and at worst a suicide run. Just enough of my mind is absorbed into these calculations and sensor checks to allow myself to really think.

Maybe I can figure out what the damn dreams mean. Not the regular ones, not the ones about me still being with Sharon. I just can't shake those memories, not even this far away. I thought I could escape, but no, I just get these new even weirder dreams, just as we passed through the mars belt. A hallucination or two if I admit it.

I'm falling and there's a hand, no a tentacle no – I just can't focus on it. Where the hell? I pop back into the navcomp, just like I never left. Crap. I was just gone forty-five minutes arguing with some something that wanted to pull me up and save me. Yeah right – save me I'm sure.

Mindless important crap has always been the way I can turn inward and look at my life. When I was a kid I used handload ammunition to zone out. If I made a mistake, I was likely to blow myself up. That kept the analytic part of my mind busy, while my emotional mind went nuts (almost literally) with the freedom to consider everything. And I'm still here. Our progressive government no longer allows such socially evil activities, so handloading would be out even if I was home. But they still let me sit console and run numbers, simulations, and cross checks. Kinda' the same thing, 'cept I can't step outside for some air, or lack thereof. And I'm not so good at avoiding these visits from my tentacle friends.

Nine hours go by and I'm just caught up. I wonder if I'm the only one who actually does the Nav work. I actually had Davidavich tell me "Я не делаю математику" (I don't do math) or close. The Russian is just simple enough that I can make most of it out. I acted like I didn't understand. I don't want the commies to think I can translate their insults. The vicious profane insults. Even they figure stuff like that transcends language barriers.

Lieutenant JG Ishikawa is scooting down the Core towards my station. I smell her long before I can see or hear her. This recycled air is another gift of our need to survive out here where we probably don't belong. But, unlike the cabbage smelling Boris crew, Yasue's olfactory announced presence is more than welcome.

"Have a good rest with computer games, Captain?"

This is rich. I'm a senior tech with the nominal rank of Captain, IE I wear railroad tracks on the uniform, but the Nihon Navy calls that a Lieutenant, 'course us/US did/does too. The Captain's sled is calling me Captain. "Yasue, it is always a pleasure to see you. Games are all finished now. Hey, you gonna' relieve me?"

"Unfortunately, no. You must remember I have essential science duties to perform. I am only here as messenger. Perhaps we will someday develop another means of more efficient communication, oops —well"

"Ok I know you are much more important member of this mission, but I can still get us all real lost, real quick. Don't think that the Borises can save you."

"Though you terrify me, I will still tell you of your good fortune. You have been bestowed the privilege of monitoring the other Greg on a repair excursion at the core base."

"When?"

"You have only thirty minutes to contemplate your great fortune. 2240 at the aft deck plate."

"You are stunningly beautiful even when you are mean." And she was. Too bad the real Captain was riding that sled.

"I accept the compliment and ignore the insult. I am genetically incapable of being mean. It is in my culture, Sempai."

"Who's my relief?"

"Abe."

"And where is Ensign Abe?"

"Just behind me. Fear not, you will not be late for your repair work. Unless I cannot trust you alone with her."

"Again, you wound me Lieutenant." She smiled and kicked hard off the back of my crash couch. "You're gonna' hurt yourself one day Yasue." At least Ensign Abe wasn't doubling up with anyone in the sleep tubes. At least that I could determine. She did take another five minutes to show up though.

"I've got your back, Lieutenant. I hope you left me with something to do."

"Not for another hour or so, when new scans are complete." Her name, Hitome suited her. She did have beautiful eyes. Damn, I have to keep that part of my brain in check. "I'll transfer to you now, if you don't mind. I have repair monitor duty in about twenty minutes, aft. And please call me Greg."

"That is difficult for me, Sempai. I do not know you so well. Besides, how could I tell you from Ensign Carlson?"

I smiled, "True, we are so much alike. Heck we're both Americans." All I got back was a return smile and those sparkling eyes. I grabbed the core rail and shoved myself aft towards the lockers to tool up. Hell, from here everything was aft.

*

Carlson was waiting for me when I got to the aft access panel.

"Greg"

"Greg"

"Sorry if I'm late."

"I don't think it's anything anyway. Our fearless leader has been acting even weirder than normal lately. Don't tell me you didn't notice. You two being so close. You being his first officer and all."

"Honestly I didn't. He's so damn creepy anyway. I just keep tryin' to irritate him and stay out of actionable shit." *Wow, did the only other American on board think I was tight with Somber Sato?* "Ya know Ensign, my friend; He has never given me any reason to suspect that I am first officer. I think he would have to die for the Borises to realize it."

"Well I know who should have been commanding this mission."

"Hell, is your nose brown – what do you know that I don't?"

"I know I am having the weirdest and most disturbing dreams of my life. I know you're having them too because the screams I hear are in clear US English."

"Hell, I'm screaming in my damn sleep?"

"Yes, Sir. And the screams are freaking me out." Nobody else bitched about it? Maybe they think it's all me."

"Anyway, what are we lookin' for?"

"The Captain says there is leakage in the thermo-couplings that cross water recycling and heat."

"And he knows this how?"

"I don't ask. That's the first officer's job."

"Thanks. OK get down in the tunnel. Ya know I'm too damn fat to get in there."

"Hey, just because you're "Big Greg" doesn't mean I should suffer."

"No, you're right. That is unfair – wait, you suffer because you are both a Tech and an Ensign."

"OK OK , I'm crawling boss."

As I lean against the bulkhead, I start to remember stuff. Thoughts that are somehow commands, and I reject them. As if I know they're just plain wrong – and too damn weird too. Were those dreams? Was I screaming? Hell if I know. But the Russians and Sato have been subdued lately. Even Davidavich let my threat go unanswered this afternoon. I didn't think anything of it then, I guess I just thought I was a big, tough American first officer. But that would just antagonize any of the Borises even more. "What ya got, Carlson?"

"Nothing yet. No moisture visible, no moisture on the instruments, Water system is optimal as is the heat pump."

"Screw it. Get back up here. If Daichi couldn't give you specifics, then we're done."

"You call him that?"

"Hell, not to his face. Tried it with Yasue once and got slapped for my trouble. I can just imagine what Sato would do. The Borises said he has ceremonial edged weapons in his locker. I'd be the crew's fresh meat for sure. You hungry for that kinda fresh meat?"

"Not yet, sir. I'll let you know, or let Sato know."

"OK wise ass. Crawl on outta there. If you weighed anything or if I could tell up from down without a sign, I'd help ya outta there"

"I do not believe you for one second, Lieutenant."

I jammed myself into the bulkhead corner near the hatchway to stabilize myself. I still kinda freaked when I just float away. "Talk to me a bit more on these dreams."

"One Nihon is having them too. I think it's Ishikawa, based on the minimal accent and female voice."

"Anybody else? I asked."

"I don't think so. Not that I heard."

"You were born in the twenties right, after Putin?"

"Yeah, you too."

"Obviously I know that. But Ishikawa's parents were living in the US during Putin. She was born on US soil after the nukes. I think she's the only foreign US first born that survived"

"Shit"

"No damn kidding Shit. The corpsman's worthless. Don't talk to him. I'll look into it – I don't know what the hell I'm looking into or why, but I will. A lot of stuff has happened to first borns after Putin. I mean we hardly get sick and we're supposed to be a bit stronger. But that makes sense. I mean 90% of us died before birth. And we got three of the remaining four thousand here on this mission. But we're different. I never consider anything coincidental with after Putin first borns"

"Yes Sir."

"Write up your report and give it to Sato. I'll talk to ya later."

"Sir", Carlson said as I left him there cleaning up. I was headed to the only private space I had. My sleep tube. I was overdue for downtime as it was.

I slipped into my tube and keyed up main comm. Arkady had the duty, "Yes, sir Lieutenant."

"I'm off shift and down. Will notify when back on deck. Don't buzz me for less than the Captain or a class two."

"Acknowledged and logged, sir. Comm out."

I fall off right away.

Suddenly I am back in Appleton. The ground is swimming with these curved pieces of meat, at least that's what it looks like to me. Hell, it's my dream, I guess it's exactly what I say it is. The meat wigglers are much deeper now, past my knees and I'm wading through 'em. Redish, with some kind of mouth, searching and biting. I kick up as many as I can and they seem agitated, at least they are moving faster and jumping higher. There's a shelf about one quarter click forward. I run for it, or rather slosh towards it, the Reds biting at me, my legs have started to ache and I fall forward into the pool of warm red slime that surrounds me.

Suddenly I'm calm, voices, lots of voices, singing to me in soft lullaby. My Grandmother is there, beckoning me down, deeper into the red. I look at her. The one human being that completely and unconditionally loved me looks back with not grayish blue eyes, but with short tentacles pulsing and angling from the sockets. This time I know I awake screaming. I lay quietly – I do not sleep.

The last mission started having innocuous communications and reports just before they reached Mars station. One week later Mars station went silent. Timing wise, we went through the same general area of the asteroid belt that Mars Seventeen traversed. We are Mars Eighteen.

I realize now that I was completely lax in any first officer duties reasonably expected of me. I followed Sato's orders even if they were bullshit because I knew that's what he wanted. I flirted with his girlfriend and did all the Borises work and thought I was this great selfless leader. I failed to notice that the rest of the crew was just one step up from zombies. Damn I hate that word, but I don't know how else to describe it. The Russians don't even argue anymore. Everybody does the minimum. No more bitchin'. No more nothing.

I have the dreams, but they stay in the background. They definitely want control. I know I know, how the hell do I know what the dreams want – but I do know.

I pass Yasue in the core. I grab her, hard. "Look I don't know if you're still in there, but if you are get in your tube and stay there until after we dock. I'll come get you then." She glares at me, but doesn't answer. And she sure as hell doesn't slap me.

I head to the armory and punch in my override codes. I just hope Sato is too far gone to notice or realize what I'm doing. I pull out three antiquated 1911's. Damn near 150 years old, but they'll work. And a laser cutting tool. I look even fatter floating down (yeah right down) towards my sleep tube. I slip in with my collection and wait.

*

The jostling of positional jets followed by a loud clank and whirring noises inform me of all I need to know.We're docked and locked. Shadows keep passing my tube. I have it tinted 85%. I can barely see anything but no one can see in. That's so much more important. I figure four minutes for the crew to clear and at least three more to figure out some of us are missing.

I pop outta my tube and key in the emergency seal code. The three sectional bulkheads slam shut and the seals reengage at the forward docking collar. No alarms like in the movies – thank heavens. All I need now are alarms.

I belt in at the helm and jerk us off station. Carlson is coming up behind me and my firing of the positioning jets slam his head against the core.

"Thanks ass hole"

"No problem, You can thank me again later. Get up here and grab a 1911. Just make sure you only hit SOFT targets. We can't hole the ship."

152

"Hey, I'm not an idiot just because we got the same name."

"Hopefully you won't find anyone, except maybe Yasue."

A voice echoes from further aft in the core, "I'll even let you guys call me that now. Save me one of those Colts."

*

I couldn't be happier. Well I guess I could, but under the circumstances at least it was three for home. And only 27 hours to the next communications window. I think I'll let the science expert handle that duty.

Neoteric Urban Archaeology
By James Van Pelt

The weird beer can should have tipped me off, but I didn't recognize its significance until later.

First, under a blanket in the corner, so caked with dirt and mold that it peeled up like rotted plywood, I found a magazine treasure trove. For a neoteric urban archaeologist like me, magazines, newspapers and old mail date the strata, providing a rough timeline for the other artifacts. Every artifact, including a faded magazine, tells a story.

Six *Sports Afield*, pages stuck together, cover images discolored, and the stack smelling of extended rot. None with subscription labels. The house had been abandoned since 2001. Gas, water and electricity cut off, windows boarded, like many other houses in the neighborhood.

Sports Afield? From where I squatted in the corner of what used to be a living room, through the broken front door, the afternoon sun scorched asphalt and cement. Beyond that, a skyline of warehouses and smokestacks. You'd have to drive for twenty miles to escape the city's center, and another twenty before you could find a decent field. That's a story! Some long-term squatter, as recently as three years ago, bought an issue of *Sports Afield* whenever he or she could afford it, sat in this ruin of a house, thinking about forests and streams.

I tapped out a note on my tablet and took a picture. Behind the magazines, jammed up against the wall, lay a hypodermic needle covered with mouse droppings. Around the room, no furniture, of course, except for a musky, water stained mattress topped by an empty wine bottle. Almost no visible floor between my stack of magazines and the mattress. Layers of detritus. An archeologist's dream. Junk tells stories about people, and a vacant house attracts new stories every night. Vagabonds, the lost, the pursued, the crazed and the exiled. Teenagers sneaking in for the mattress. I'd find a lot of DNA on it if I checked. Illness too. The homeless often are undertreated.

Raw stories. Recent stories. The unwritten stories that would never be told if I didn't record them.

Once, I found a sword in a scabbard on the floor of an empty house. What was its story? I found a beautifully maintained typewriter from the 50s, a stage pistol, filled with blanks, a hundred-dollar bill inside a sock, a Barbie still in its display box, both so water stained and moldy that I couldn't immediately identify them. I found a cat's skeleton wearing a beautiful collar. The flashlight reflected from the rhinestones around the delicate neck bones.

I moved away from the magazines and sat on the mattress. A mouse scurried along the baseboard, rattling over a newspaper in its panic. A bit of pink fabric poked up from beneath a crumpled fast-food cup. A pair of panties. I recorded them in my tablet too.

People who hide use empty houses. If I wanted to drop out of view, become untraceable, I'd use vacant buildings. Perhaps I too would leave a bit of my story behind: a crumpled candy wrapper, a forgotten glove, a piece of what I'd brought but dropped.

I used my stylus to pick up a beer can, a local Texas brand they don't sell in Chicago. Someone carried that beer in a backpack or a duffle bag all those miles to be dropped here. I plucked another beer can covered with Arabic letters from the floor, and beside that rested a can I didn't recognize. Squat, no seams, and it didn't appear to be made out of aluminum. I snapped a picture, then put it in my collection basket to examine at the lab.

Would I have known what I stumbled into if I had just found the weird beer can? I don't know, but what I found under a crushed shoe box beside it brought me back to the beer can later. Under the box lay what looked sort of like a cell phone. A bit longer than normal and narrower. I find cell phones some times: cheap, throwaway ones, but I didn't recognize the make of this one, and it didn't have a screen. What it had instead was a button protected by a switch cover. I weighed the strange object in my hand. Heavy. Solid. Expensive feeling. I slid the cover aside and pushed the button.

It buzzed, or hummed. For a second, I thought a lightning bolt lit the room, or a flash from a camera. I blinked and covered my eyes because the light continued, blaring. My eyes teared, and I realized it was sunlight. I was sitting in sun light on what was left of the mattress. Half of the house, where the cell phone had been pointed, had vanished. In its place a shallow crater that extended to the front yard, and the sidewalk too, a perfectly clean cut.

A police car drove by. The officers didn't look my way. Behind me, the building creaked as it listed a foot to one side. I thought it was going to collapse, but it stood. I took my finger off the device's button.

Now, I sit at my desk in my apartment, the strange beer can and the cell phone resting in front of me. They are made of the same, odd material. They must have been dropped in the house, left, I think, by accident, like everything else.

Found objects tell a story. To an archaeologist, even a broken shard, a bit of writing, a thrown-away tool reveals the lives of the occupants. They are narratives. For a neoteric urban archaeologist like myself, the stories are about temporary people. The invisible ones. But I'm having trouble with this story. There's nothing earth-like about the beer can's metal. There's nothing familiar about the . . . what? . . . ray gun?

Who stayed in that empty house? Where is he now? Where was he from?

Yes, that's the question, and the answer that will give me the story: where was he . . . she . . . it . . . from?

The Next Step in the Dance
by Maureen Bowden

They say he fled the sea and led them in the dance.
Perchance he walked the waves or called them to his aid.
Afraid, the old ones were, who fed him to the tide,
They tried to dim his light and turn their heads away.
They say he fled the sea and led them in the dance.

Across the land he danced and every step she shared.
Each word upon the wind she kept within her heart.
Apart but locked in love they waited for their time.
The rhyme and rhythm of the surf upon the sand,
across the land he danced, and every step she shared.
                (Ancient Poem from the annals of the land of Greca)

Theo was born wrong. That's what we believed. He would tilt his head, as if listening, and smile at what only he could hear. He would stretch out his hand for something that wasn't there, and whatever he'd been reaching for, a book, a candle, or maybe his favourite toy, a painted wooden snake, would appear in his grasp. I felt uncomfortable in his presence. If he approached me I would step backwards, only to find him standing beside me. All the children avoided him, except Phaia, my baby sister. She would hold out her arms and run to him. He would kneel, and pull her into his embrace. She giggled and spoke to him in semi-formed, infant chatter. He understood, and replied. They sat together, in conversation, the six-year-old boy and the two-year-old girl.

My grandmother, Cloe, was the village wise-woman. "What's wrong with Theo, Grandam?" I asked her, as we walked together along the beach.

She pointed to a pool amidst the moss-covered rocks. "Look into the water, Alexi, and tell me what you see."

"Tiny creatures," I said.

"Are they alive?"

"Yes."

She pointed to the shoreline, where our pet dogs, Leda and Calypso, were running and splashing in the breakers. "What do you see?"

"Animals."

"Are they alive?"

"Yes."

"Are you and I also alive?"

"Of course. But what does this have to do with Theo?"

"Life is a dance," she said. "Each step must be learned. The rock pool creatures can't run and bark, and play on the sand. The dogs can, but they're unable to speak, and reason, and create tools or things of beauty. We can do these things, but Theo can also hear distant sounds, call objects to his hand, and move as fast as light. He's taken the next step in the dance."

"Should I fear him?"

"Phaia doesn't. Be guided by her."

The fisherman, Bain, was lounging on the sand, his nets left unattended at the water's edge. I didn't like him. All the villagers played their part in providing food and shelter for everyone, but although I was not yet ten years old I worked harder than he did. I turned to Cloe. "There's one that missed a couple of dance steps, Grandam. He belongs in the rock pool slime."

Cloe grinned. "You have a tongue as sharp as a fish knife, Alexi, but don't make an enemy of that man. He's lazy and stupid, but dangerous."

Bain was afraid of Theo, and his fear turned to hate. He gathered the young men around him and his hatred infected them.

At low tide the remnants of an ancient forest poked through the exposed seabed. One of the tree corpses resembled a gnarled hand with crooked fingers stretching landwards. We called it the claw. The old people told of a time when enemies of the village were bound to it with ropes, and left to drown when the sea came in. That was many years ago, before we made peace with our enemies. Such things were now no more than stories to frighten children, who laughed away their terror in the safety of their parents' arms. Bain was about to revive the old ways.

It was almost dawn when Phaia shook me awake. Her agitated babble made no sense to me, but she too had taken another step in the dance, and she placed her thoughts in my head. Bain and his friends had made their plans by passing notes to each other so that Theo wouldn't hear them and be warned. They'd taken him in his sleep, dragged him to the shoreline and bound him to the claw. The tide would turn at dawn and the sea would take him. I was about to call to my parents, but Phaia placed her finger on my lips. Her voice in my head said, "He says you must tell no one. They won't help." I knew he'd told her the truth. Apart from Cloe and this tiny girl, all the villagers would be relieved to see him die, because he was different. She handed me the knife our father used for skinning fish. "Save him," she said.

I pulled on my leggings, climbed through my bedroom window, and ran faster than I'd ever run in my life. I reached him as the waves were surging around his waist. I could see bruises on his arms and shoulders and his hair was matted with blood. My rage gave me strength to hack through the ropes that bound him. He wrapped his arms around me, and before I could blink the salt water out of my eyes we were safe among the rocks beyond the high tide line.

He held out his hands and dry clothes appeared in them. He dressed in silence before turning to me. "Thank you, Alexi. Now I must go away."

"You can't," I said. "Phaia's heart will break."

"She knows that I'll come back for her when the time's right."

"I'll come with you," I said. "I can't go home. Many of the villagers will be awake by now. If they see me they'll know it was me who set you free. I'll be the next one Bain ties to the claw."

"They won't see you." He gripped my arm and we were standing outside my window. "Phaia needs you. Be kind to her." He reached into the air and a painted wooden snake appeared in his hand. I looked at the small child with his favourite toy, and my eyes filled with tears. He smiled, turned away from me, and disappeared.

I climbed through the window. Phaia was sitting on my bed. She took the knife from my hand.

Word spread through the village. The young men strutted and sneered and claimed to have rid us of a monster. At low tide Cloe walked to the claw, returned carrying the severed ropes, and flung them at Bain's feet. "You're a fool," she said, "and that little boy, wherever he is now, is no monster. He's the first of many such children. Will you try to murder them all?" She let her gaze wander over the rest of them. They wouldn't meet her eyes and they moved away from Bain, disassociating themselves from him.

Nobody found out who set Theo free and as Bain became more and more isolated no questions were asked. I confided in Cloe. She laid her wrinkled hand upon my cheek. "You did well, Alexi. Now you must do as the child asked. Be kind to Phaia."

"Theo's so young and he's alone. Do you think he'll be all right, Grandam?"

"I can't tell you for certain, but I believe Phaia will know of any harm that befalls him, and she'll turn to you for comfort. If she seems content, so is he."

Within the next three years five babies in our village, and many in other villages, developed the ability to hear distant voices, move objects without touching them, and travel at great speed. Some, like Phaia, could speak without words. When Bain's own daughter was found to have the power to see through solid objects, he left the village, walked to the claw and waited for the tide to turn. Nobody tried to stop him.

It was fifteen years before Theo returned. I knew he was coming when Phaia, now a beautiful young woman, packed a satchel and stored it under her bed.

"Are you planning to leave?" I asked.

"Yes," she said.

"With Theo?"

"Yes."

I sought out Cloe. "Theo's coming for Phaia. Our parents will try to keep her here. What should I do?"

"I'll speak with them. They won't stop her. Neither must you."

"I'll miss her, Grandam."

"I know, Alexi, but she and Theo must live their lives together and you must make your own life. Find a mate, and have children. She doesn't need you now. Let her go."

He waited for her at the edge of the village. Cloe and I watched her walk to meet him. I raised my arm to wave to them and a painted wooden snake appeared in my grasp. Phaia's voice in my head said, "For your first child."

They turned away from us. She took his hand, and then they were gone.

Piper's Haunt
By Maureen Bowden

The ancient standing stone in the meadow alongside our farm, pointed, like a bony finger, to the sky. I could see it from my bedroom window.

"Why is it called Piper's Haunt?" I asked my father, when I was no more than six years old.

"There's an old story, Will," he said. "Long ago, a magical being, the Piper, walked the land. When the children heard his music they rose from their beds and followed him to the Otherworld, where they laugh and play and stay young forever." He took me on his knee, and I snuggled against his chest. "One of the children was afflicted, and couldn't run fast enough to keep up with them. The portal to the Otherworld closed before he could reach it. When the Piper counted the children, he realised that one was missing, so every full moon he returns to the standing stone and waits for a child to make up the number."

"Is that why mamas and papas tell their children to be good, or they'll sell them to the Piper?"

"Yes. It's said that he'll leave a child's weight in gold at the foot of the stone, in exchange for a son or daughter."

"Would you sell me or Maggie or baby Ned?"

He laughed. "No, Will, don't worry. You're all worth more to Mama and me than any amount of riches."

I didn't worry. We had no need of gold. The harvest was plentiful and the farm thrived. Maggie, Ned and I grew plump and healthy, and life was good. That was before the sickness came upon me.

Our troubles started two years later, the day Ned fell into the duck pond. He was only three years old and the water was deeper than his height. Not realising the danger, Maggie and I laughed, as the ducks quacked and scattered, and he yelled, in his baby talk, "Help. My is cold." We stopped laughing when the waves lapped over his head. I jumped in and hauled him out.

Mama changed his clothes, gave him a cup of hot, sweetened

milk, and warned him, "Don't you go frightening the ducks like that again, my boy, or I'll give you a good spanking."

Maggie giggled, "You'll be joining the Red Buttocks Clan, Neddy."

"My won't," Ned said, draining his cup and running off to find more mischief.

Mama hugged me. "Thank you, Will. You saved your little brother's life." I felt warm inside, but that night I couldn't stop shivering.

Next morning my head ached, my arms and legs had lost their strength and I coughed so bad it hurt my chest. Mama gave me a herbal potion to ease my head, and she made me stay indoors.

Weeks passed and I didn't recover. "He needs fresh air," Mama said. "It may help to clear his lungs." I was too weak to play in the farmyard with Maggie and Ned, so Papa carried me on his shoulders and we walked the farm's boundaries.

"This is a good place to live, isn't it, Papa?" I said.

"Yes, son. Mama and I have made it so. We only value what we have if we've worked hard to get it."

"I wish I could help, but I'm too weak. What use am I?"

"You're a good lad, Will, and I know you'll always do whatever you can. That's all anyone can ask of you, and it's all you can ask of yourself."

He stopped to rest at the edge of the meadow where Piper's Haunt stood. I noticed a shadow in the far hedge. It looked like a dark entrance to a cave. I pointed. "What's that, Papa?"

"I don't see anything," he said.

"Look, there. It's an opening in the hedge."

"No, Son. It must be a trick of the light, deceiving your eyes." I knew he was wrong.

My illness grew worse. One day I sat, wrapped in a blanket, on the doorstep while Maggie and Ned played Catch-a-Ball. They threw the ball towards me, trying to include me in the game. I reached for it but a coughing fit overcame me and I tasted blood in my mouth.

Mama put me to bed, and Papa saddled his horse and rode five miles to Glastonbridge, the nearest town. He returned with Master

Joseph, the medic, who examined the bloodstained handkerchief Mama showed him. He tapped my chest and my back, and made me take deep breaths, although it hurt. They left my bedroom and I listened through the open door, as they talked downstairs.

Master Joseph said, "William has the lung sickness. I'll give you a linctus to relieve his pain and help him to sleep easy through the night."

"Will he recover, Master?" Papa said.

"I'm sorry. There's nothing more I can do. He won't live to reach manhood."

I buried my head in my pillow and wept.

One night, sweet music drifted through my dreams. The melody painted pictures in my mind, of dust motes dancing in a sunbeam; snowflakes settling on a winter bare-boned tree; and a piper playing in the moonlight. It held a promise of eternal childhood, and freedom from pain. I awoke. A full moon shone into my bedroom and the music played on. Compelled by its call, I slid out of bed, and crawled to the window. I looked out and saw him, leaning against the stone, the pipes to his lips. The moon lit a silver path towards the gap in the hedge. He set his feet upon it, and began swaying and skipping across the meadow as he played. Nothing mattered to me except to follow him. I tried to stand but my legs wouldn't bear my weight. I dragged myself on my hands and knees to my bedroom door, but Mama heard me. She carried me back to bed and stayed with me until I drifted into a dreamless sleep.

The next morning I said to my parents, "I know I'm dying. Give me to the Piper so that I can be well again, and stay young in the Otherworld."

Mama took my hand and shook her head. "The Piper isn't real, Will. He only exists in an old story."

"But I saw him, I saw the portal to the Otherworld, and I heard the pipes."

Papa said, "Sometimes, when we're ill, our dreams seem real. We'll make you well. Good country air and fresh food is all you need. Rest now, and forget the Piper."

The following year a drought came upon the land and the harvest failed. We had nothing to sell, and my parents had to use their savings to buy fresh fruit and vegetables imported from far off provinces, to feed us.

"All will be well next year," Papa said, but the lines in his forehead and around his eyes had deepened, and Mama grew thin and tired.

One day a stranger came to the door. Papa stepped outside to speak with him. I was sitting close to the window and I saw Maggie creep from the side of the house to where she could overhear their conversation. After the stranger left Papa came back inside with some papers in his hand. He passed them to Mama and shook his head.

When the evening chill made it hard for me to breathe, Mama carried me to bed and stoked the hot coals in the fireplace. Later, Maggie brought me my supper.

"Who was the man who spoke to Papa?" I said.

"No one for you to worry about."

"I'll worry more if you don't tell me, and don't lie. I know we have troubles."

She sighed, and sat on the edge of my bed. "He was from the bank that gave Mama and Papa a mortgage on the farm. We have no money left to pay it." Her voice trembled. I reached out to her and we clung to each other. "If we don't settle the debt within a month the bank will take everything. We'll lose our home and there's nothing we can do about it."

"There is," I said. "Are you strong enough to carry me?"

"Of course I am, I'm nearly a woman, but why? Where do you want to go?"

"On the night of the next full moon take me to Piper's Haunt."

Her face paled. "You believe the Piper's real?"

"I know he is. I've seen him."

She shook her head. "I can't do it, Will. I'm sorry."

"Listen, Maggie. I'm not strong enough to work for money to help save the farm, but Papa once told me he knew I'd do whatever I could. I can do this. The Piper will leave my weight in gold." I hugged her, and forced myself to laugh. "I know I don't weigh much but it should be more than enough to pay the bank."

She kissed the top of my head. "We love you, Will. We wouldn't want you to sacrifice yourself for us."

"It's for me, too. The Piper's music promised that I'd be strong and happy in the Otherworld forever. I want that. If I stay here I'll die."

"What if you're wrong, and it's not real?"

"Then you can come back to the stone next morning and bring me home."

"You can't ask me to do this. Mama and Papa would never forgive me."

"Then persuade them that it's what I really want. It's the only chance for all of us. I'm not strong enough to argue with them, but you are."

She nodded, but tears stained her cheeks. "I'll try."

I don't know what she said to them but they listened. At sunset on the night of the full moon, Papa carried me to Piper's Haunt. Mama, Maggie and Ned came too. Papa laid me down by the stone and Mama covered me with a warm blanket. "We'll be here at sunrise, Will," she said. "If the Piper hasn't taken you we'll carry you safely home."

I nodded. "If I'm not here you'll know I'm well and happy, and you won't have to worry about me anymore." My family kissed me goodbye and turned away, crying.

I fell asleep as the sun melted below the treetops, and I awoke to the Piper's melody when the full moon shone. He stepped from behind the stone and onto the bright path that led to the open portal. I threw off Mama's blanket and crawled after him. Pain tore through my chest and I fought for every breath, but the pipes drew me on, and I dragged myself across the cool meadow grass. He reached the opening in the hedge. Beyond, I could see sunlit fields stretching towards snow-capped peaks on the horizon. Children were playing on the banks of a fast-flowing mountain stream, bathing their toes and tossing pebbles into the silver-flecked water. My strength was almost gone and the portal was starting to close, but he stretched out his hand and I grasped it. Life flowed through me. The pain subsided. I rose to my feet, and breathed the fresh night air. Glancing over my shoulder at the standing stone, I saw the Piper's gold gleaming in the moonlight. I turned back to him, and together we passed through the portal. The hedge closed behind us, and I ran, laughing, in the sunshine.

Retirement
by Beth Powers

My husband was dead. This wasn't the way it was supposed to work. That's why we'd waited until the war ended to marry—so we could live happily in retirement—not so I could bury and mourn him alone.

He'd deserted his army (it had never been his cause), and my side couldn't afford to acknowledge what I had done to put the queen back on her throne. So when the peace was signed, before the thumbchip readings were even logged on the seal, we'd disappeared, married, and lost ourselves among the fringe worlds.

We'd been on this barren ball of dirt for more than two years, and it was almost beginning to feel like home. We'd bought a little house, nestled among a small cluster of settlers, far enough from either of our birth planets that we were convinced no one would ever think to look for us here.

I discovered how wrong we were when the colonial police showed up at my door, saying there had been an accident, a malfunction in Warren's gravcar. It had thought a brick wall was open road. He was dead.

Thanking the officer, I closed the door. Straight to my bedroom, I dove under the bed. It took some finagling, but I managed to release the catch and reached into the hidden compartment. I emptied its contents and headed for the front door.

Slapping the opener with my free hand, I found a neighbor about to press the buzzer with something that smelled freshly baked under her arm. "Mona, what are you doing?" she asked with alarm, fixing wide eyes on the gun.

I jammed the powercell in place, "I'm going to hurt someone."

She put a hand on my arm, "That won't bring him back, Mona."

"Don't—touch—me," I rasped.

"He's dead," she dropped her hand, "You can't solve this with a gun."

"Says who?"

"He's gone, Mona."

"I know that." I tucked the gun into my belt. "I can't bring him back. Noted. But somebody's gonna pay." The gun would only be back up. Breaking them into tiny pieces with my bare hands would be significantly more satisfying.

"This isn't the way to handle it," my neighbor insisted.

"You're right," I told her before shutting the door in her face. I spent the next three weeks trying to find a target, someone responsible. Neighbors showed up on the doorstep, looking worried, and explained that GalEnT officers from the port city had arrived to investigate the mechanical malfunction. If anything else was going on, they insisted, GalEnT would find it. I took their comfort food and listened to their words with empty ears as I sat cycling through enemies and motivations, trying to figure out who wanted Warren dead.

I didn't share their blind faith in the self-styled Galactic Enforcers of the Law. I'd clashed with GalEnT a time or two while running one of the most active cells in the Vamirran underground. They were something akin to a protection racket transitioning into a legitimate law enforcement agency, but I wasn't impressed. They excelled at puffing their own reputation throughout the galaxy, but I'd never found much teeth beneath the myth. Instead of awaiting the results of their investigation, I let the mountains of sympathy-food grow until my kitchen smelled like rot rather than a bakery, and I continued my search for someone to kill.

Warren found me first. Three weeks after he died he came limping down the lone paved road that ran through our settlement.

He was my husband, and I had buried him. Nothing could have prepared me for seeing him alive again. I had been sitting on the front porch to get away from the smell of spoiled food in the kitchen, and I looked up to see Warren, whole and hale, living and breathing. Setting aside the datascreen I'd been studying, I stood stiffly. My mind completely shut down. At first, I could do nothing but blink in disbelief. No matter how many times I closed my eyes, he was still there in the blinding sunlight, battered but alive, limping slowly toward our house.

Before my mind had finished processing, my feet flew down the steps. I was quicker than Warren and he stopped his slow progress when he saw me coming. As he shaded his eyes from the sun, that easy grin that I had thought I would never see again spread across his face and glinted in his eyes.

As reality caught up with a sudden fear on its tail, I came to an abrupt halt a few feet from him. Stretching out one trembling hand, I laid it against his chest. He winced slightly as though my light touch was painful, but didn't step back. My hand met solid and felt the beating of his heart underneath. No ghost, no demon, no dream.

I traded my hand for my head and buried my face in his dust-covered shirt. Warren put his arms around me and breathed into my hair. Closing my eyes, I murmured into his arm, "If you weren't already dead, I'd kill you for scaring me like that."

His only reply was to sigh contentedly and whisper back, "Ah, Mona, I missed you."

I managed to get him inside before any of the nosy neighbors noticed. He wrinkled his nose at the smell, but didn't make any jokes about my cooking.

I went to the kitchen to make some instant kri, but I'd seen his face—it was bruised and in need of a shave, but not marred by scratches from the pavement. I had assumed that he bailed out of the gravcar when it went haywire. But if that was the case, he should have been more banged up. "How is it you didn't die?" I held out the cup of steaming liquid.

He chuckled, took the cup, and caught my wrist, pulling me into his lap. "I wasn't in the gravcar."

My eyes narrowed, "Just where were you?"

Warren set down the cup and rubbed a hand over his face. "Okay. But first you have to promise not to grab a gun and hunt someone."

I kissed him on the nose, "I'm staying right here."

"I never made it to the gravcar. I was picked up first," Warren explained. "They were looking for you." He grimaced.

My anger boiled over and I attempted to jump up, but Warren was ready for me. The chair toppled sideways, and we both landed on the floor. Warren wheezed and flipped over onto his back. "Thanks, Mona, my ribs were getting a bored with all of the sitting."

I rolled to my feet and held out my hand to him. "It's your own fault."

Warren waved my offered hand away. "I'll stay here. Thanks. It's safer."

"Fine." I righted the chair and sat on it. "Tell me what really happened."

"I don't know," Warren shook his head. "They didn't take the time to introduce themselves. They also didn't kill me and they asked about you."

"Why not just pick me up instead?" I reasoned, "I was right here."

"I'm not sure they realized that," Warren frowned, "Or maybe they did. It's all a little fuzzy."

"Sounds like my enemies then, not yours."

"Probably," he agreed.

His enemies would have been easier. Pretty much the only people who cared about cannon fodder who deserted the army were the ones who wanted to throw them in front of the cannon. And that side had lost the war, so the higher-ups had bigger concerns than one soldier who vanished during guard duty. I, on the other hand, had been on several most wanted lists for leading an active and high profile cell of the Vamirran underground. I liked to think my team had something to do with which side won the war, and there were a lot of folks in the galaxy who weren't too happy about that.

"And you have no idea what they wanted?"

His answer was interrupted by the door buzzing. Someone must have seen us in the street. I stabbed my finger onto the opener fully prepared to throw whatever food was offered in the giver's face. I was not, however, prepared to find GalEnT on my front porch. The woman was dressed in a blindingly yellow uniform with a matching beret that made sure no one could overlook the fact that GalEnT was on the scene.

"Mrs. Baine, I'd like a word with you."

"If this is about my husband, I've nothing to say," I responded, reaching out to shut the door.

"I know you're probably still digesting how delicate life can be, but I think you'll want to listen to what I'm about to say," her tone held an underlying threat, and she took a half a step forward, so that if I wanted the door to slam in her face, I would have to push her backward to get her out of the automatic sensors.

"What's GalEnT doing investigating a mechanical malfunction?" I asked abruptly, resting my hand on the doorframe to block her from advancing. I would have never suspected GalEnT in this—I was thinking it had to be one faction or the other of Vamirrans. Third party interests never crossed my mind.

She smiled, as though I was a child that had just solved a difficult problem. "I've no need to investigate. We wanted you to fully understand the nature of the situation before we asked you to come and work for us. We like to recruit talent where we see it, but we understand the need for a person to be properly motivated."

"Are you a profiler, Agent—" I read the name on her uniform, "—Smith?"

"No, we have people who do that."

"Well, you'd better fire your people because if they told you this was the best way to get my cooperation, they were wrong." Without looking, I keyed a code above the opener, and the door whooshed shut, causing the woman to jump back to avoid getting smashed.

Warren stood just out of sight in the kitchen. "They used me to find you," he observed quietly. "I should have—"

"No," I cut him off, resting my hand on his arm and meeting his eyes, so he would know I was serious, "It's better we do this together." No way was I going to have my husband feel bad for coming back to me. Besides, it saved me the trouble of hunting them.

Warren squeezed my hand in acknowledgement and headed for our bedroom. I was already turning toward the large floral painting hanging above the couch when someone—probably the woman— began scraping at the front door, undoubtedly trying to get it open. I ignored it, grabbed the painting with both hands, and tossed it aside. I almost felt sentimental about some of the knickknacks we had picked up in the spaceport on our last stop to moving here, but not that painting. I'd always hated the washed out colors. Flowers should have more life to them.

Behind the painting hung a wall safe. My fingers danced across the keypad as I deliberately entered the wrong code. There was nothing in the safe anyway. The only thing in this house that I cared about was walking toward me with two backpacks that we had filled with supplies and a small arsenal of firearms long ago. Handing one to me, he hit the opener on the door leading to the garage just as they started shooting. I could hear a faint beeping as the door closed automatically behind us, and I smiled.

I opened the side door while Warren fired up the gravcycle. Pulling a rifle from the rack on the wall, I swung up behind as he drove past. I only had to lay down cover fire for a few seconds before our home of two years exploded behind us, sending a wash of color into the night sky.

*

Warren slid the bike around a curve down the road that led to both of the major cities on our colony world. The capital would allow us to lose ourselves in the masses, but the port city would give us access to the stars. "Where to, Des?" his voice sounded in my ear through the mike that linked our helmets. "Your call."

My heart stopped for long enough that Warren called back, "You still with me, Des?" in a concerned voice.

There it was again. No mistake. I patted him on the back and waved my arm around in front of him to signal a request to pull over as though my helmet mike wasn't transmitting correctly.

He complied and I stepped off the cycle as calmly as I could, removing my helmet. He did the same, holding out his open hand, "Want me to take a look?" he offered. An easy smile lit the face that I loved; the face that I thought I'd never see again.

I threw the helmet at that face, trying to smash it. I didn't wait for the outcome, but swept my foot out to hook his ankles and dump him in the dust on the edge of the road. He offered no resistance as I strode forward and placed my boot on his throat. "Who are you, and what have you done with my husband?"

"What are you talking about?" he wheezed, trying to catch his breath. The confusion in his eyes and voice seemed genuine.

I ignored the single tear tracking down my face. He looked exactly like Warren would, down to the tilt of the head, but I knew it wasn't him.

"Only one person persists in calling me Des"—I preferred Mona—"And it's not my husband."

He shrugged it off, "So my brain's still a little scrambled. So what? It's me." He held out his right hand, "Read my thumbchip if you need proof."

Instead of responding, I reached down and removed his sidearm, tucking it into the back of my waistband. "If you move, I will shoot you." Fake-Warren or no, he would hear the promise in my voice. Slipping out of the straps, I opened the pack I had been carrying.

As I searched for one of the items in our emergency kit, I talked. "You know thumbchipping is an ineffective system, right? Law enforcement knows it, governments know it. I know it. So don't insult my intelligence. If I want to be you, I remove your thumbchip and put it in my thumb. Or I reprogram mine. To the electronic world, I'm you." I found the small flat square designed to look like a handheld mirror. "More importantly, the Vamirran imposter's faction knew that. Perhaps she cared more because she was trying to take a throne that wasn't hers. Anyway, her armies experimented with different methods of identification." I activated the device. "One was to inject her soldiers with a substance that would spread throughout the body, allowing it to be identified with a simple scanner." I held the mirror over his feet. The lights across the bottom remained a steady blue. "My husband was one of the test subjects. And you are not him," I finished, although I continued to move the mirror up the length of his body.

"What are you talking about?"

His response surprised me. I would have expected Warren to call my bluff. Warren would know that there was no such thing as what I had just described—too many people liked the loopholes in thumbchipping—but this wasn't Warren, and I would have expected an impostor to at least hesitate.

It didn't matter if he believed me; he only needed to stay put for a few more seconds. So, I continued, "You may as well tell me who you are. I'll find out soon enough."

As I moved the scanner toward his head, he insisted, "But I remember you. I remember when we met—how I ended up on your ship by accident—how you and your team thought I was dead—how you wouldn't let them kill me, you said it wasn't my fault for being in the wrong place at the wrong time."

If he had tried, he could have knocked me down with a feather. "How do you know that? What did you do to him that you have his memories?" Science could do wonderful things but to my knowledge memory implantation wasn't one of them.

"I didn't do anything to him—me—what was that?" he asked as my device beeped, and data began streaming across the mirror.

At first it didn't make sense. Then, I realized I had been wrong. I'd been looking for some sort of listening device that would let me trace those working with the impostor, those who killed my husband. But the device picked up a complex transmission, and the numbers told me that my husband was alive, lying in the dirt at my feet.

I pulled the gun from my waistband, flipped it to stun, and shot him in the chest.

Not having much understanding of electronics, I wasn't sure what I was seeing on the device, but I did understand its basic operation, and it was telling me that whatever was transmitting from Warren was receiving far more data than it was sending out. I realized there was another reason he might call me by the wrong name—if he wasn't the only one in his head. I didn't know if such a thing was possible, but it gave me hope.

Even better, my device had a strong lock on the signal, which meant I could find the source. I just needed to get Warren there. I pulled out a new comm (I'd left my old one to be destroyed with the house) and pressed the emergency button.

When the emergency gravcar arrived, I waited for the paramedics to get Warren on a hoverstretch and into the back before I stunned them both and climbed into the front of the vehicle. It had been awhile, but I discovered I hadn't lost my ability to override the automatic controls and drive manually. Using the signal as my guide, I headed for the port city.

I knew from past encounters that GalEnT frequently operated out of office buildings, so I wasn't surprised when the device led me to a looming silver structure with hundreds of windows. On the hoverstretch, Warren was easy enough to transport into the building. Outside the suite of offices, I picked up the rifle that I had laid next to Warren and used it to smash through the frosted full-length plastic next to the door.

If it had ever been office space, the cubicles had been removed to be replaced by electronic equipment, including a chair holding Agent Smith, minus the beret, with a silver halo around her head. Two men in labcoats skittered backward like roaches at the sight of my rifle. I traded the rifle for the handgun and stunned Agent Smith for good measure, although I assumed I had cut off her eyes and ears when I stunned Warren.

I turned to the scientists, "Whatever you did to him, undo it."

"We didn't do-do anything," one stammered, edging toward the room's comm.

"Wrong answer." I shot him in the leg. Ignoring his screams, I turned to the other one, "How about you?"

"You don't understand, it's a delicate procedure. We implanted-"

"Good point." I powered the gun down to stun and shot them both. "I don't want you mucking about in my husband's brain anyway."

I rummaged through my pack again until I found a small pen-like device. When I hit the power button, it let out a low hum and vibrated slightly under my fingers. Using the mirror scanner, I pinpointed the location of the signal, tracing it to the side of Warren's neck. I couldn't see anything, but I hoped whatever they had put in Warren was electronic and touched the pen to his skin. I felt the electricity crackle up my arm, and Warren's eyes flew open, "What was that?"

"What's my name?"

He gave me such a puzzled look that I thought he wouldn't answer, but finally, he said, "Mona." Then added slowly, "Why?"

I continued to frown at him because hijacked-Warren had known things too, and I couldn't think of a way for him to prove that he was himself.

Without losing the puzzled expression, Warren sat up, saying distractedly, "Where are we? Did I call you Des? I never do that. Mona?" When I didn't answer, he turned back to me. "Mona, you shot me. What's going on?"

I didn't answer him until I had removed Agent Smith from the chair. "I shorted out the device that she was using to, I don't know, not control you exactly, but to use you somehow to steer me where she wanted."

"I don't remember that," he looked at me with wide, scared eyes.

"Don't worry," I patted him on the arm, "As soon as we take care of this, I'm taking you to someone I trust to get that tech out of your head."

"She's not dead?" he asked with surprise, looking at Agent Smith sprawled on the floor.

"Do you know how big GalEnT is? Killing her would solve nothing."

He laughed at me, and I smiled, satisfied that I had him back. For now. But he asked seriously, "What do you plan to do with her?"

I glared at the woman who thought I would want to work for an organization that threatened the man I loved. "Oh, I have an idea."

*

Outside, I stood next to the hoverstretch with Warren by my side. I could hear the fire alarm ringing through the building behind me. Agent Smith slowly opened her eyes and struggled to sit up. The other two were tied up in the back of the emergency vehicle. "You certainly have our attention, Mrs. Baine," Agent Smith hadn't lost any of her crisp professionalism, "I am authorized to give you considerable incentives if you agree to work for us."

I fiddled with the datascreen in my hands, "You don't understand, Agent Smith. I'm not interested in working for GalEnT—or anyone."

Agent Smith shook her head as though scolding a persistently stubborn child, "It is you who doesn't understand. It is a professional courtesy that we are offering you anything. Eventually, we won't give you a choice."

"Hmmm," was my only response, but I could feel Warren laughing through the hand he placed on my shoulder. I handed Agent Smith the datascreen tuned to a local newschannel.

I watched the color drain from her face as she watched herself badmouth GalEnT and her superiors before taking credit for blowing up their lab. As it turned out, GalEnT's people were good at labeling things and keeping prototypes that didn't require surgery to function. "No one will believe this," she told me, almost sounding like she believed herself.

I shrugged, "Even if they don't, GalEnT isn't going to be happy with you for losing control of their technology. It's the end of your career either way."

She glared at me, opening her mouth, undoubtedly to say something along the lines of "We'll get you in the end."

But I interrupted, "I know GalEnT will send someone else—another Agent Smith or perhaps an Agent Jones—and I'll admit, you caught me by surprise this time, but next time—if they can find us, that is—I'll be ready and I'll destroy whoever they send. And the next one. And the next. Or you could save your superiors the trouble and expense by passing on this message: *I'm retired.*"

Above us, an explosion tore through one of the offices, raining dust and debris down on me and my husband as we walked away, hand in hand, toward the spaceport where we could lose ourselves among the stars.

The Tulku of Titan
By Mike Morgan

"The ashes blew straight up," repeated Sonam quietly, "as if they were caught in a vortex. There is no clearer sign than that."

The wind was whispering softly as the committee of High Lamas meditated on the shores of the lake. Sonam should have been relaxing into that meditation along with the rest of the committee, but his thoughts were restless, colored with anxiety. No, it was more than anxiety: it was dread.

"Yes," replied Yonten sadly, sitting cross-legged to his left and equally failing to meditate. "It was only a matter of time."

"And the Oracle couldn't get any clear sense of him here on Earth," Sonam continued, the words slipping from the corner of his mouth.

From his position in front of them, Saragarhi turned his head and regarded the pair sourly, all meditative quiescence gone. "Your minds seem scattered today, brothers. But you may calm yourselves. I have had the vision that we seek."

Sonam asked in surprise, "You have? Already?"

Saragarhi nodded. Gently, he added, "Tell me Sonam, do you enjoy long journeys?"

"You know I do not," answered the lama.

Saragarhi let out a sigh. "Then I fear you will not like what I saw."

Sonam felt the dread settle about his shoulders, bearing down on him like a dead weight. "Is the tulku we seek so very far away?"

Yonten muttered crossly, "You know how contrary Gendun Gyatso could be. He even said before he died that he'd use his phowa as a way of protesting what's happening here in Nepal."

Sonam ignored Yonten and stared beseechingly at Saragarhi. "Tell me," he pleaded.

The older lama replied serenely, "My vision was of an orange moon orbiting Saturn."

"No," exhaled Sonam, before he could stop himself.

Saragarhi continued, "And of a small metal thing that floated near it. The metal place looked very old, almost worn out, I'd say."

"Getting there is going to cost a packet," spat Sonam.

Saragarhi had the cheek to simply shrug in response to the financial objection. "We must go where we must. The days when we searched only in the local region are long gone."

Yonten interjected diplomatically. "I'll get some pictures of the moons of Saturn. Let's see if our brother can identify which one he saw in his vision." He smiled beatifically. "Once we have the moon pinned down, it should be relatively straightforward to establish what station we need to visit."

The lama stood up slowly, his aged joints stiff. "Don't fret, Sonam. I'm sure the flight won't last more than a year. Eighteen months, tops."

*

Molly Douglas was trying to get Oli to nap when Commander Hanover called. With her three-year-old child shrieking in the background, she answered the line.

"Molly? Sorry to disturb you, but something rather important has come up." She found she couldn't quite tell what expression was on Hanover's face in the small image projected by the wall-mounted communicator. He looked as amused as he was panicked, the two conflicting feelings warring for territory on his features.

"Is there an issue with a flight plan?" she asked, confused. "I'm off shift right now, but I suppose I can come in if you need me in Control. I'll have to get hold of Maureen to watch Oli for a while, but--"

"No, it's nothing to do with work," interrupted Hanover. "All the traffic you were tracking prior to end of shift is fine." He paused, "Actually, the inbound cargo transporter docked already. The, ah, people who want to see you were on it."

"People?" she queried, changing mental gears rapidly.

"Yes. Well, I say people, but 'delegation' might be a better term for them." He smiled nervously. "You don't mind if they drop by, do you? I'll pop along with them, just so you know there's nothing fishy going on."

Molly didn't know what to say. "Oli is meant to be taking a nap," she began, but then she realized the station commander was going to arrive in her cabin in just a few minutes and the cramped confines of her living quarters were a cluttered, toy-strewn mess.

"We won't keep you for long," replied Hanover, bulldozing his way through her feeble argument. "And they've come a long way to see Oli."

"Oli?' squeaked Molly in disbelief, but Hanover had already hung up.

*

Molly made tea for the Buddhist lamas. It seemed like the right thing to do; although, on reflection, it was probably the wrong type of tea.

Twenty minutes notice had barely been enough time to shove toys into the under-bed storage bins and straighten the sheets. There was still a pile of dirty dishes in the tiny galley's sink.

There were three men in the Buddhist delegation; each one was stooped and wiry, dressed in robes of dark crimson and golden yellow, with tall hats shaped like rooster combs. The color of their hats and under-robes wasn't entirely dissimilar to the light orange atmosphere of the moon the station was orbiting.

They introduced themselves, in faltering Standard, as Sonam, Yonten, and Saragarhi. Apparently, there should have been more than three of them--there should have been an entire committee and a gaggle of officials--but space travel was enormously expensive and they'd been forced to economize.

Given the limited amount of space available in her single-room cabin, the three lamas were perched on the edge of Molly's bed while the commander occupied one of the bar stools at the breakfast counter. Oli was racing around, bouncing off people's legs and reveling in the opportunity not to nap.

While she waited for the kettle to boil, Molly attempted conversation. "We don't see many outfits like those on Titanville. You sure won't be hard to miss while you're staying here. What do you call those? Robes?" They were sure different from Oli's plain unisex coveralls and Molly's lightweight pants and tunic.

"Yes," answered the one who'd introduced himself as Yonten.

The middle lama, who looked a little younger, muttered something disgustedly about not having ceremonial clothes with them on account of not being able to afford the increased luggage weight.

Yonten made a tiny gesture and the other Buddhist clammed up; strangely, they had an air of naughty schoolboys trying to be on their best behavior. They were also clearly very interested in Oli.

The oldest of the lamas asked Hanover with a piercing glare, "And you're sure no other child was born on the date we specified?"

Hanover shrugged. "Titanville has a population of exactly four thousand six hundred and twelve permanent residents, and since we're all cooped up in the same tin can, it's kind of easy to keep track. So, yeah, I can say with absolute authority that you're looking at precisely the only kid born on August fifteenth or on any day near then: little Oli Douglas."

The lamas went back to staring at Oli. The kettle boiled loudly.

*

"You think Oli might be the Dalai Lama," repeated Molly stridently.

She nearly poured the hot tea right over the elderly Buddhist, but steadied her aim just in time. The second his cup was full, she put the pot back down on the counter, not trusting herself with it anymore.

"The Dalai Lama is a type of bodhisattva called a tulku. He is able to reincarnate by choice. During his phowa, his transfer of consciousness, he can decide how he is to reincarnate. This time, we think he may have chosen here," explained Yonten.

Molly struggled to recall the details of the Dalai Lama's passing. Titanville was a long way out, but the Earth news still reached them even if it did arrive a few weeks late. "Didn't he die, what, three years back or thereabouts?"

"Yes," said Sonam heavily. "That's right."

She got the point; Oli's birth coincided with the Dalai Lama's passing. "This is ridiculous," she protested. "We're not Buddhists. And Titanville is a shabby, forty-year-old hydrocarbon processing plant left over from the start of the twenty-third century. Everything here has seen better days. Your leader isn't going to want to be born into any place like this."

Hanover interrupted, "They have a test they want to perform. It won't hurt Oli. They already talked me through what they want to do, and there's nothing dangerous involved. Can they go ahead?"

Molly pursed her lips. "If you think it's fine, I guess so. They have come all the way from Tibet."

The most wrinkled of all the lamas, Saragarhi, corrected her as he pulled a small bundle out from the folds of his robe. "We had to leave Tibet over two centuries ago. These days we are based in Nepal, but I think our association with that country might be coming to an end soon too. The country is a dictatorship and the government is interfering in our religion just as the Chinese did in Tibet."

Saragarhi finished unwrapping the bundle. In the open folds of the material, six small items were revealed. Molly could see some keys, a necklace, a statue of a bird, and some other jewelry. They looked like personal effects.

The lama called softly to Oli to come take a look. Oli hesitantly tiptoed over and peered at the objects.

Sonam said quietly, "Oli, two of these things are yours. Can you pick them out? We'd like to give them back to you."

The child's hands flashed, and before Molly could blink, the key and the tiny bird statue were gone from the collection of items.

"That's right," said Yonten. "Thank you, Gyatso."

*

"So what's next? Oli's the head of a major religion, all of a sudden?" sighed Molly, wishing she had something strong to slip into her tea.

"Next, the child will be shown to three associates of the Dalai Lama to confirm his identity," announced Saragarhi. "The selection of the correct personal items was merely a first step."

Molly's eyes almost popped out of their sockets. "Now you just hold on there, pal. Oli's not going anywhere! Certainly not Earth!"

Sonam's mouth fell open. "But the Dalai Lama must be trained in a monastery. He has to go to Nepal--"

Yonten abruptly said, "Are you sure? We're about to be forced out of there. Perhaps it is not wise to bring the reincarnated Dalai Lama into such a dangerous situation."

Saragarhi considered the point, eventually replying, "Many of our teachings are spread through electronic communications nowadays. It's not inconceivable that a Dalai Lama could be trained off-Earth and spend much of his time out here. He would still have the same impact on followers throughout the Solar System."

He peered at Oli, adding, "With so many people leaving Earth and moving to the Outer Worlds, is that what you intended? That we should look to the future, and move somewhere we will not be oppressed?"

Oli said, "I like ice cream and penguins!"

Molly raised a hand to get their attention. "Excuse me, but you've said 'he' a couple of times now. I think there's been a bit of a misunderstanding."

Saragarhi shook his head, bemused. "There is no misunderstanding. Oli is short for Oliver, is it not?"

Molly winced. "It is sometimes. In this case, it's short for Olivia."

Sonam started laughing, and it wasn't long before Yonten and Saragarhi joined in. "That removes any lingering doubt," gasped the youngest of the three lamas. "Being in space wasn't enough for Gendun Gyatso; naturally, he would only settle for also reincarnating as the first female Dalai Lama."

He wiped tears from his eyes and stood up from the bed. "Miss Douglas, we'll see you bright and early in the morning. Olivia will be a good student, I hope."

Pick up more Alban Lake titles at
http://store.albanlake.com

Pick up more Nomadic Delirium titles at
http://www.nomadicdeliriumpress.com/blog/sh
op

www.ingramcontent.com/pod-product-compliance
Lightning Source LLC
Chambersburg PA
CBHW051514170626
46811CB00002B/827

* 9 7 8 0 9 8 6 3 7 0 5 5 7 *